The Crash Crystal

A LEGO® Mystery

A Middle-Grade Novel for 9-12 Year-Olds

By John D. Wagner

www.CrashCrystal.com

ISBN 9-781-46807944-9

Printed in the USA

02 03 04 05 06 07 08 09

Author photo: Alyse Volino © 2012
Waving Monster: Micah Wagner © 2012
Book design: John D. Wagner

For Leita

For Micah & Asa

CONTENTS

Chapter One

A Simple Man's Grin

"Oh Mack, come on, you're not going to bring that crystal, are you?" my Dad asked. "You and Evers and the silly stuff in his attic. We'll never be rid of it."

At first, I thought he was kidding.

"What's that, Jake?" my Mom asked, as she walked up the stairs with a suitcase.

"Everett's crystal," Dad said, "It's right there in his back pocket."

"Well," my Mom said, "if he feels like he needs it, honestly, what's wrong with that?"

Dad and I were packing for a trip...on *very* short notice. My Aunt A.D. had just called, somehow getting my Dad's cell phone and our home phone to ring at the same time. I'd watched Dad out of the corner of my eye as he scrambled to answer. He had been *pretending* to read the newspaper, although he was *actually* watching my newest YouTube Lego video. That's a hobby of mine, making those, teaching kids the cool stuff I know.

When he answered his cell, he didn't even finish saying, "A.D. hi…" when he let out a groaning, "Oh no."

Then he fell silent, just listening.

Something seriously bad had happened. I could just feel it.

I stood right next to my Dad, waiting, until he finally cupped the phone and whispered to me: *It's your Grandad; it's Evers. He's very sick.*

"And where is he now?" Dad spoke into the phone.

He paused.

"Well," Dad sighed, "we knew this was coming. It was just a matter of when. Okay, I'll…I'll drive down tonight," he said. "I'll get there around midnight, depending on the ferry. You don't have to wait up, A.D."

He winced, like he had a headache, and said, "Do you think this is it for him, A.D.? It's lucky he made it to 80, really."

He hung up and called upstairs to Mom. Then he turned to me, when I asked what the heck was really going on.

"Remember when Grandpa Evers was so sick last summer?" Dad said. But he didn't finish his sentence, because Mom had appeared in the hallway.

"That was A.D. on the phone," he said to her, "It's not good. It's Evers. Looks like he's in a coma."

Mom instantly got her *concerned mom* face on.

"I've got to leave tonight," Dad said. "But wow, it's late to start out…"

"Why not take Mack?" Mom said. "He can miss school."

"Yeah, he can miss school!" I said, talking about myself.

Mom shot me a look and continued, calmly saying, "Plus, if Evers is that sick, it may be the last time Mack sees him. He can say his goodbyes."

Goodbyes? Why would they be talking so calmly about someone who was dying?

"Well," Dad said, turning to me – recognizing it was a good idea to take me along – "just so you understand what we're walking into, Mack. Your Grandad is probably in his last hours. He won't even recognize you. You're ready for that?"

I nodded *yes*, but I wasn't really sure. First, I didn't want Dad to go alone. Neither did my Mom. Plus, as freaky as it would be to see someone in a coma for the first time ever in my twelve years of life, I was thinking of something else that had nothing to do with Evers, even though I didn't want to admit it. You see, Dad's laptop has an excellent mobile broadband connection – government-issued, actually. It's the same network the President uses, because my Dad's a Federal airplane crash investigator. He carries a badge and everything. He'd probably let me cruise the Web in the car for the whole ride down. You know, MineCraft, Miniclip, Lego.com. That's something I can do at home only on weekends, if you can even believe how unfair that is.

"O.K. then, let's do it. Pack for three days away, Mack," Dad said, snapping me to action.

For just three days? Pack what? Like, why bring anything? I thought.

I wandered into the hallway with just my toothbrush…and a few required items in my pocket.

"Where's your suitcase? Where are your cloths?" Mom asked.

I pointed to what I was wearing, with a look that said: "What the heck, this ain't enough?"

But then Dad appeared at the bottom of the stairs, distracting Mom.

"A.D. said something really odd," Dad said out loud to no one in particular. "She said Evers is unresponsive, but he's lying there with *a grin* on his face."

"A grin?" my Mom asked. "That's eerie."

"A grin. That's what she said," Dad explained as he climbed the stairs, tossing me some clothes to throw in a bag.

As for why I was even bringing my crystal, all I know is that *someone* had put it out for me to pack, right on my pillow. The way Dad was acting, I figured it must have been Mom.

Grandpa Evers had given me that crystal about a year ago, the last time I saw him, when we'd met in the attic where – under strict lock and key – he kept his special things, his collections. It's my favorite place in his house. Actually it was my favorite place just about *anywhere*. The crystal is a bright rose-red color, but it isn't that big, really. About the size of a candy bar. Or half of a candy bar, I should say, because whenever I looked at it, I got this strange feeling that it was half of something larger.

Now, here's the thing: Mom wanted me to take the crystal this time, but she didn't *always* feel that way. So, I was going to cut her some slack and not mention it. She'd said that a crystal can draw certain powers…maybe even the wrong powers. Mom's like that, a little bit of a worrier. Sometimes she needs like a gallon of herbal tea just to go to sleep.

As for my Dad, ever since I got the crystal, any time he saw me tucking it into special places, he chuckled, saying stuff I thought he shouldn't say about his own Dad. Once, when he didn't know I was listening, I even heard him say to Mom that Evers was "just a loopy, old coot." Kinda bothered me, because I'd never talk about *my* Dad that way.

Well, we packed up, and Dad and I started driving to make the last ferry. Without Mom there to tell us to slow down, we went like eight-five miles per hour the whole way, *and* we stopped to eat at Mickey Ds – that's McDonald's in case you didn't know. Another Mom no-no.

Sure enough, Dad's laptop and Internet connection came *very* handy for passing the time. Thing is, Dad turned real quiet once we started driving. A little spooky. But he didn't even check what websites I was on. Major score.

We made the ferry, and once we docked at Martha's Vineyard, we drove over to Grandpa Evers' house. He'd lived there for a long time, way before my Grand-mama died (I never even met her). Evers' children – my Dad and my Aunt A.D. – hadn't lived with Evers since *they* were kids, until last year when A.D. moved back with Evers, because he'd turned 80 years old and needed help.

A.D. had waited up for us and right away gave me a huge hug. For someone as old as she is, which is like 40, she's *way* cool. She wears different colored Chucky-T high-top sneakers, and two or three tie-dyed T-shirts at once. Plus, *tons* of silver bracelets that go way up her wrists. She has short hair, like a boy's, all spiked up, but then she has a long thin braid, like the natives in *Avatar,* and that goes all the way down her back. There are actual gemstones woven into her braid. Kinda hard to shampoo, right? Oh yeah, and she has six silver hoop earrings in one ear! *Six.* To top it off, she plays the trombone at all hours. She says it doesn't bother the neighbors nearly as much as her last instrument, the Scottish bagpipes.

"Mack, I'm *so* glad you're here," she said, "You can help take care of *all* of us."

Then, she turned to Dad, and they hugged silently. She was crying, for sure, and I think Dad was too, but maybe not, because I didn't have a perfect view.

"It's strange," A.D. finally said with a sniffle. "It just doesn't seem like he's dying, not with that grin on his face…"

"You're sure it's a grin. He's not in pain?" Dad asked. "I mean, it's weird, even for Evers. You gotta admit."

"It's definitely a grin," she said without hesitation. "And what do you mean by a comment like *it's weird even for Evers*?"

My Dad looked away for a sec, and then at me.

"Can we even go see him?" I asked to break up a brewing argument.

We walked into Evers' room, and A.D. hugged my shoulder, because she knew I'd be freaked. I'd seen one dead person before, at a wake. Way creepy, with the casket open and everything; the person's skin was like wax. But now it wasn't exactly the same. First of all, Evers wasn't exactly dead. And sure enough, he *was* grinning! Just lying there on his bed, his eyes closed, flat on his back, looking happy as a man in the middle of a good dream.

"Told ya," A.D. said to my Dad.

"Oh good God," Dad said in muttered astonishment.

"He looks like the Buddha," I said, "he looks just like the Sleeping Buddha."

We had a statue of the Sleeping Buddha at home. That's how I know. It's Mom's.

A.D. turned toward me and said, "You know, that's right. He *does* look like the Sleeping Buddha."

I couldn't believe we were talking like that in front of someone who was dying.

Dad looked quietly at Evers for a long time, before saying: "Well, let's just keep him comfortable. Nothing more we can do, is there?"

We headed off to our bedrooms. Dad put me in the sunroom in a hammock, but I lasted five minutes there after I spotted something very spooky. It was a Lego figure that looked like it might have been left out just for me, and I ended dragging my sleeping bag back into Dad's room. Before you call me a scaredy-cat, let me drop *you* in a strange hammock with a half-dead guy in the next room and see how long you last. Plus, when I called Mom just before I went to sleep to tell her that Dad and I were OK, something weird happened.

"Oh good," was all she said over and over when she picked up the phone. "Oh good. Glad you're safe."

She sounded sleepy. It was, after all, like 1:30 am. A late-night record for me, except for the last two New Years.

Then, so Dad wouldn't hear, I whispered into the phone: "Mom, thanks for putting the crystal out on my pillow. You know, to remind me to pack it."

"What?!" she said, suddenly very awake.

There was a weird silence that made me wonder if we got disconnected.

"What did you say?" Mom asked, in a voice that gave me goose bumps. "I didn't put the crystal out for you, Mack. What are you talking about? Mack? Are you there? Is Dad right there? Are you safe?"

Chapter Two

Mysterious Movements

"Pancakes!" Aunt A.D. shouted. Her voice roused me from down the hall.

I opened my eyes and looked around, a little stumped at first. I was expecting to see my own room, with my Lego At-At walkers lined up on my bookshelf.

Then I remembered I wasn't at home.

So, I rolled over to look for Dad. But I started swinging wildly back and forth and almost fell out of the darn…hammock?

I was back in sunroom!

Someone had moved me during the night after I'd gone to Dad's room.

I reached into my pocket, and it was still there. No, not the crystal. That has its own special pouch in my duffle bag. The thing I was checking for was the key, Evers' key…the one he'd given me to the attic.

You see, all his life, Grandpa Evers' collected *tons* of stuff from Southeast Asia. (Where's that? Google Map it dude. I had to.) But he stored it all up in the attic, probably to keep from scaring any kids who might come to visit. Not me, of course. Littler kids. Like, actual children. But here's the thing.

Although Evers' house has a regular lock, the attic has another lock, as I said. You'd double-lock this stuff too, if you saw what he was trying to keep safe up there. Bludgeons. Blood-stained Indian swords. Sacred skulls. That sort of stuff. Sometimes I swear the lock wasn't meant to keep people out, but to keep Evers' collection from *escaping*.

"Oh, here we go with another jungle adventure. Indiana Jones, the remake," my Dad would say whenever Evers tried to explain what was up there, kind of making fun of him.

That *had* to hurt Evers' feelings. Just sayin'.

But it wasn't just knives and swords and skulls that were in the attic. And actually, maybe Dad would feel different if he just took some time to listen to Evers, because the really cool stuff up there was what Evers called *talisman*... spiritual-type things that are hard to explain. Luckily, I'm an expert, so I can tell you all about them.

A talisman might be, like, a dried-up monkey's fist clutching a sacred gem. Creepy, I know, but maybe that's the point. Or it could be a rare bird's feather that's been somehow lanced through a stone. No matter what, a talisman can have strange powers to take you to another time and place just by touching it. Or by wearing it. Or even by just having it nearby.

"This is real witch doctor stuff," Evers would say with a sly smile, whenever we examined his collection together, wrapping and unwrapping each item in purple felt. His favorite talisman was a carving of a bird that was bursting free of a stone, where you could hardly tell where the stone ended and the bird began.

"The stone symbolizes our physical natures," Evers explained when he first showed me the carving. "But the bird is the spirit striving to break out, to be free. It's a remarkably consistent image in all human cultures."

Now, as I lay there in the hammock wondering how I got there, I could practically hear Evers' voice and see his eyes glistening, as he held the bird talisman in front of me, asking, "Which are you drawn to Mack, the earth or the heavens?"

"Um, the heavens, I think," I'd said, not really sure what he was talking about.

"Talisman may be strange to you," Evers had said, sensing that I didn't really get it, "but Mack, just think how exotic your Legos would be to a Tibetan tribesman. You may have talisman in your life already. It doesn't have to come from a tribe or a priest. It can be, well... look here."

He pointed to a Lego airplane I'd made.

"This could be your talisman. Just by holding it, you could be taken to another place, to another range of knowledge and ability."

It didn't seem likely, but I had cut him some slack and didn't say anything. That all happened last summer, the last time I saw Evers.

I swung out of the hammock and walked into the kitchen. As A.D. made a racket with the pots and pans cooking breakfast, all I could really do was eye up the attic stairway, waiting to make a break for it. Fact is, I wasn't really hungry for breakfast, partly because it seemed very odd that we'd be eating pancakes and having a grand old time with real Vermont maple syrup, when Evers was dying in the next room. Call me crazy.

"Who moved me back to the sunroom last night?" I asked, as I chomped down on a pancake.

"You woke up back in the sunroom?" A.D. said, a bit surprised. "Must have been your Dad."

Dad walked in just then, saying good morning.

"Dad, did you move me back to the sunroom?" I asked.

"Not me," Dad said.

Everything grew really quiet for a sec, and Dad and A.D. looked down, pretending nothing was wrong, like I wouldn't even notice.

A.D. turned to me and said, "Sweetie, I know it seems a little spooky, but maybe you were just sleepwalking…"

Oh come on, I thought: Sleepwalking as I climbed out of my sleeping bag, down the hall, into a swinging hammock and back into my sleeping bag? Not very likely, Aunty A.

Then Dad started to tell a story that A.D. obviously didn't want him to tell.

"There has always been something about that sunroom," he said. "A.D. always heads there when she needs to check in with the spirits. Didn't do much for us when we were buying lottery tickets, but hey, if it works for you…"

Dad was half-smiling, in a teasing sort of way. But A.D. wasn't exactly smiling.

My Dad went on: "Once, Evers was lost off the coast of… where was it, A.D.?"

"Sumatra," A.D. said, cleaning blueberries, and never looking up.

"Right, Sumatra," Dad said. "And he was with his friend. What was that guy's name?"

"Roland," A.D. said, again, determined to keep her answers short.

"Roland, *right*. Wow, he was Dad's ideal traveling companion… spooky, kooky…the full package," Dad said. "A.D. went into that room to mediate for a while and came out saying Evers would be fine. How'd you know that, A.D.?" Dad asked, suddenly serious. "You've never explained that one."

"Well, my little brother," A.D. said with a sigh. "There's a beautiful order to things in this life. An elegance. That's something you have always refused to acknowledge, because things take different forms than you expect."

Then she looked at me and winked, saying, "Seems odd, but it's true."

Just maybe I understood what she was talking about.

I was still eyeing the attic stairway, waiting for an opening.

I thought A.D. was done and I started to get up, but she started talking again, foiling my escape.

"It's really not hard to explain," she said, pointing to the steam disappearing from the teapot.

"That water in the teapot is very real. You can touch it," A.D. said. "But then it turns to steam and disappears. So, does the water exist any more? Of course it does. It's just in another form."

A.D. took a pinch of air and flicked it at me; I swear I felt a tiny splash on my face.

"I checked on Evers through the night," she said, as she cooked. "He's still got that grin. Weirdest thing, isn't it? Grinning at a time like this."

"A.D." I said, with a question that came out of nowhere, even for me, especially since I was actually trying to escape the room. "How did my Grand-mama die?"

A.D. looked a little surprised.

"Mack, she got suddenly sick and died when your Dad and I were young," A.D. said. "We were kids, really, around your age."

"But of *what?*" I said almost angrily. "I mean, people have to die of something! And was that part of some big cosmic plan?"

"Mack, looking back now," Dad said, "it was probably a very strong flu. Evers wasn't even here when our Mom first got sick. He was coming back from one of his crazy trips to Thailand."

A.D. reached over and smoothed my hair and said, "She's here now, you know, your Grand-mama. *Right here*," she said, pointing to my heart. She was about to say something more when Dad interrupted her.

"Mack," Dad said, "why don't you go unpack real quick in the room where I have my stuff?"

I got the hint and headed to Dad's room, turning my eyes real quick to see Evers lying there, as I walked down the hall. Was that a key just like mine on a string around his neck? I got to the room and reached into my bag, and that's when I realized that the rose crystal was missing!

I knew for a fact it was missing and not just lost in my bag, because I'd wrapped it in velvet with a rubber band. Well, the velvet was there. And the rubber band was there.

But no crystal.

"My crystal's gone!" I shouted as I charged back into the kitchen.

"Which crystal?" Aunt A.D. asked.

"Evers' crystal. My crystal. My personal property. The one he gave me!" I said.

"Oh, you've misplaced it…" she started to say. But I cut her off, because, oh man, I was mad.

"*No*, I didn't, misplace anything," I said.

A.D. and Dad gave each other another one of those knowing looks.

And like I wouldn't even notice, A.D.'s arms had goosebumps. Those goosebumps got even more obvious when I told her why I'd gotten so spooked and left the sunroom last night.

"It had something to do with this!" I said, as I pulled out a Lego sculpture of a bird, half bursting into flight.

"Where'd you find that? Did you make that?" A.D. asked. I shook my head no.

"Jake, is that yours?" A.D. asked. He shook his head no as well, looking mystified.

"I saw it last night for the first time in the sunroom," I said. "Someone had left it there. For me. Someone made it just for me."

"Evers?" my Dad said, looking up the hall toward his room.

Kind of impossible when you think about it. If Evers made it, he would have known I was coming. But how could he? And how could he know I'd find it in that room?

Whoever made that must have been able to tell the future, don't you think? It was more than just weird. It was weird times ten thousand, actually. What was going on?

With that, we all heard Evers make a sound from the next room. Not a groan. More like a sigh; a long *ahhhhh*.

Chapter Three

Swords in the Attic

A.D. and Dad walked in to check on Evers, but I scrambled up the attic stairs, digging for my key, and in three seconds I was at the door.

My key worked perfectly, and I went right for the rack of Evers' tribal swords, the big curved ones. I can't tell you how long I've waited to get my hands on these with no grownups around. Turns out, I was very lucky to be holding those swords, because no sooner had I grabbed them than masked warriors were coming at me with swords of their own. *The classic ambush I've long prepared for!* It was all I could do to fend them off, slashing wildly at the air.

And what's that? More attackers in the shadows? I spun, barely escaping their deadly blows. *A bit unfair gentlemen, wouldn't you say, distracted as I am by my Grandad's coma?* I ducked just in time, slashing, and my sword went clunk, sinking deep into an attic rafter. Oops, maybe that was a little too real. Man these things are sharp!

Oh but look at what we have here, lurking in the corner. If it isn't my old arch-enemy come to see me, Harry the Foul, a.k.a. Sir Duffus. That's actually a kid from my school. I only *wish* he were there to duel me, now that I finally had the swords.

He real name is Harry Doney. But I call him Harry Donkey. He was *so pissed* the first time he heard that nickname, he attacked me with a ski pole. Harry is actually quite skilled at the art of the ambush; I'll give him that. He somehow times his attacks *perfectly*. When teachers hear a commotion in the schoolyard, they always look up *after* Harry has struck. They just see me fighting back. And they punish *me*! Which I'm sure you'll agree is completely unfair. More like a crime actually.

I'm kind of kidding when I say I want to duel with Harry. What I *really* wish is that Harry could have seen me and Evers working on the tribal stuff in the attic, when Evers was healthy. Then he could see Evers handing me special knives, using museum-type language and Harry would recognize the many, many things I am already an expert on.

"Mack," Evers would say, handing me a tribal knife. "Let's label this one as a weapon from the Boer War. Note that there are human blood stains on the tip and base."

"That's the Transvaal War, right?" I'd say – like Harry would even know what that was.

"Precisely. 1880. South Africa," Evers would say matter-of-factly," his half glasses perched on the end of his nose.

And if Harry managed to overcome his cowering fear of knives and skulls, and actually say something, it would be, "Could I… maybe, could I maybe hold that knife?"

Evers and I would look up and raise our eyebrows, and then talk a bit quietly between ourselves. I'd sigh and say, "Sorry, Harry, I don't know if you really should. This is pretty serious stuff we're dealing with here. Things you wouldn't understand. And I'd hate to be responsible if anything bad happened…"

I'd told that story to Mom, thinking she'd love it, but she said it was "small" of me to think up stuff like that. Still, if Harry ever saw all these knives, and knew for a fact that they would be my own personal property when I turned 16 – as Evers promised in front of my Dad, so he's a witness – I'm sure he'd regret his little ski pole stabbing incident, if you get my meaning.

The closest I came to making Harry realize all the stuff I knew about tribal weapons was when we had a Display-Describe Day at school. Display-Describe Day – which I call triple D – is basically "Show & Tell," but we *begged* our teacher Mrs. Reilly to change the name, because it's not like we were kindergarteners showing off our Thomas the Tank Engines.

For a triple D last year, Evers let me bring an actual Gurkha knife to school, and of course, I packed my rose crystal too. As I unsheathed the knife – man, it was *huge*, the blade etched with war scenes – Harry was the *only* one in class who wasn't impressed. Or he pretended not to be. I starting out telling the class all about the Nepalese Gurkhas, who were the toughest fighters on earth.

"And this same Gurkha knife could very well have been used to defend a real king's life in battle," I said, pointing out stains on the blade. "That's probably human neck blood right there," I said.

Nearly everyone was wide-eyed in amazement. Even Mrs. Reilly gasped. Everyone, that is, except Harry, who said, "What a load! Who'd believe that?" as he looked around for other doubters to help mock me out.

Luckily, Carly – she's just a friend of mine, definitely not a girlfriend of mine, just a regular friend-friend who just *happens* to be a girl – spun around and said, "*I* believe it. And Harry, maybe you should give Mack a chance to tell the story before you…"

Then Mrs. Reilly stepped in and gave her usual speech about extending the same courtesy to the presenter that we would expect for ourselves. Being the presenter, I agreed with her. For once.

When I started talking again, Carly winked at me, and that's when it hit me that Carly was really a younger version of my Aunt A.D. A mini A.D. Only without the haircut or the bracelets. But *with* the Chucky T's, plus Carly also wore different-colored shirts one on top of another, just like A.D. Kind of freaky now that I got a chance to think about it.

After Mrs. Reilly warned Harry, I decided to bring out
the crystal. I mean, talk about saving the best for last! I started to
tell the class what Evers had told me when he opened his exotic
treasure trunk and pulled the crustal out before giving it to
me…about how a young monk named Krit had given it to him,
but that Evers wanted me to have the crystal just in case anything
ever happened to him, *and* that I had to be careful because the
crystal was very powerful, *and* that the crystal's powers would
reveal themselves *only if* the crystal were in the hands of the right
person, *and* that Evers thought maybe that person was me.

"What is that a time-travel telephone?" Harry said. "Why
don't you give that to your Dad so he doesn't even have to go to
the airplane crashes? He could call back in time to warn the
pilot. Hey, how much is that thing worth? Can we sell it on eBay
and buy Legos?"

"That'll be enough of that, Harry!" Mrs. Reilly shouted,
and with that the class broke up before I could really tell the full
story. Even though that was last Spring, it stilled bugged the
heck out of me.

Now, with Evers downstairs and A.D. and Dad looking
in on him, I stood there staring at the very trunk that originally
held the crystal. Should I open it? Evers wasn't going to appear
at the door to stop me. I decided to look inside.

I expected to have to pry it open, but the lid seemed
weightless…and there, on a top of piece of velvet, I saw

something that the hair on the back of my neck stand up: It was my rose crystal. The same one that went missing from my bag.

It sat next to an old photo of Grand-mama and one of Evers in a temple somewhere, smiling with the same grin he had on his face downstairs. The way the pictures were placed, both Grand-mama and Evers seemed to be looking right at me.

I actually lost my breath. I couldn't even yell for help. I know I couldn't yell for help, because I tried. And tried.

I grabbed my swords again and spun, slashing at the air, trying to keep away the spirits that were surely right over me, *for real* this time.

I reached in to take the crystal back, but I suddenly had the feeling that I had to snatch it, to actually steal it, because just then, all by itself, the lid slowly started to close. I grabbed my crystal and then – boom, boom, boom – three things happened all at once:

The lid of the chest fell with a thud.

A.D. yelled out, *"No!"* two floors below, and…

Grandpa Evers took his last breath.

Chapter Four

First Crash

Evers always said that he wanted half his ashes spread in the Ganges River in India and half in the Atlanta Ocean near his house. But after he was cremated – that's when they burn the body, in case you didn't know – it seemed to me that going all the way to India to scatter ashes was a bit of a trip for Mom and Dad, so I was already Googling how legal it was to mail a batch. Turns out it's not legal at all, and looks like people are kind of picky about it. Go figure.

A week after Evers died, we gathered with his friends at Aquinnah beach. The service wasn't sad for me, probably because I was practically right there when Evers died. I could hardly believe that just days ago I'd run down from the attic into Evers' room to see my Dad sobbing. Which made me cry, just seeing that. Aunt A.D. was biting her lower lip to keep from crying, too. She forced a smile when she saw me and again pulled my head close to her chest, saying over and over, "You're so special to us, so special…"

Listening to stories about Evers at the memorial service – and his ashes were like two feet from me in an urn, so that proves that I wasn't even scared – you had to agree that the dude was a serious wild man. Don't believe me? See how many actual Buddhist monks show up to help throw your ashes in the ocean. Evers scored *three*, one who sat right in my row, all dressed in orange robes. Weird, but his eyes widened with surprised when I brought out the rose crystal to hold during the service. He leaned toward me and looked as though he wanted to snatch it. Mom asked me to put it away, before I caused an international religious incident.

After the service, A.D. took the lid off Evers' urn, and a wind gust whipped the ashes into a cloud that gently fell into the nearby waves.

"We'd better find a different spot to go swimming after lunch," was all my Mom could say.

When we drove back to our real home after the memorial service, I just wanted to flop out and watch TV. But suddenly, almost like it was timed, Dad's pager went off with the piercing *whoop, whoop, whoop* signal…from the NTSB, the agency Dad works for that tries to figure out crashes. A plane had gone down and his Go-Team was being mobilized, on the double. I actually felt kinda sorry for Dad. Mom did too. After all, didn't anyone notice that his father had just died? And here they were making him flying to a crash site the day after the funeral.

"And life goes on," was all Dad could say as he dashed out the door to meet his driver and get over to his jet.

Whenever my Dad was called to a crash site, I always went online to read about it and watch any YouTube clips I could find showing where he was. As I said, before I really grew up and turned twelve, I wasn't allowed to spend more than thirty minutes online at any one time. Sometimes I didn't get the Internet *at all* during the week… just on Saturdays and Sundays. But since I changed schools, and I needed the web for homework (*thank you* for once homework!), I could go online almost as much as I wanted. "Within reason," Mom had said.

But even when I was doing my homework, I *did* sneak in a little Dragon Gamez and Miniclip, when no one was watching. Oh, and Lego.com. And more YouTube. And Facebook. And Minecraft. And…well, you get the idea. That's within reason, right? Still, when Dad is away with work, and Mom catches me spending too much time on the web, we have a fairly typical conversation that goes like this.

"Sweetie, I want you off the computer!" She says.

"But there's nothing to do," I say.

"You have 10,000 Lego pieces. Build something!" She says. And she's right. I do have *tons* of Lego pieces. But they get boring, because once you've put together a huge Lego project and you play with the finished pieces for a few days, it gets a little old. So, I break the projects up and make totally different kinds of space ships and planes. When I have those done, I make Lego landing bases, some as big as my bed. No kidding. I have so many Legos, I can invent totally new Lego creations. And trust me, these are things that the head honchos at Lego haven't even dreamed of.

In fact, when I've got *tons* of time, I clear off the junk from a section of my bedroom floor – Magic cards and D&D stuff mostly – and lay out my Lego pieces in a certain order. Then, I reassemble them and make stop-action videos with my video camera, showing how I built my latest models. These are the videos I told you about that I put on YouTube, and I get *tons* of hits! It's like having my own Lego TV station. I think most of the people watching my videos are kids, but I'm sure the top Lego engineers watch too. One day, I'll see some of my own original concepts for sale on store shelves. I'm sure it's coming.

Anyway, when I Googled the crash that my Dad just went to investigate, I didn't find much on the web, only that it was a cargo plane that had lost power. It fell from just 200 feet. Still, 60 tons dropping from 200 feet makes a real mess. There were no passengers, and the two pilots survived. The pictures of the wreckage didn't tell me much either, since all plane crashes look the same – horrible. But then, on Google Images, I looked for a picture of the type of plane that crashed, and I stumbled across photos of the two pilots. An electric feeling rippled through me when I looked at their eyes. It was almost as though they were looking back just at me, telling me something, telling me to do something. I somehow knew them.

I suddenly dashed up to my room, because I had an almost uncontrollable urge to build a Lego scene of the plane and the crash site. As I worked, grabbing Lego after Lego, it was as though my hands were being guided. The more I worked, the more obsessed I was to get every detail just right. I looked up when I'd finished the plane and saw it had gotten dark outside. That was odd, because the sun beams exactly through my windows right at sunset, lighting up the room, but I didn't even notice. With my plane perfectly assembled – and I have to admit it was some of my best Lego work ever – I worked to recreate the crash site on my floor, with all the runways and buildings in the same places I saw on the web.

When I'd finally finished the Lego plane, I backed up into the hallway outside my room, so I could glide in for my runway approach.

"What's you doing?" Mom said as she made her way up the stairs with a laundry basket.

"Making Legos," I said. "Just flying my planes. Hey, was that Dad who called before? Did he figure out the crash?"

"Well, not yet," Mom said, "it doesn't seem to be a fuel problem, but it's a mystery, because *something* made both engines fail at exactly the same time. Dad said the plane barely got off the runaway before it crashed."

After listening to Mom, and zooming my plane around some more, it became real clear to me why the plane crashed.

Not only that, but I was convinced, *really convinced* that both the engines from the crashed plane still actually worked fine. I don't know *how* I knew that, but I couldn't get the idea out of my head. I just knew I was right.

I burst back into the hallway.

"Mom!" I yelled.

"Don't yell for me, sweetie, come and find me," she yelled back.

I sprinted down the stairs.

"Mom, I've solved that crash. The one where Dad is," I said.

"Well, we all have our theories, Mack," she said, "But Dad's the expert...and "

She stopped suddenly and stared at me. But she wasn't staring at the plane I made, best Lego assembly maybe ever. She was staring at my crystal, which I was clutching in my hand.

"It's *not* a theory Mom. I *actually know,*" I said. "Go call Dad. Just call him. Tell him my idea, and you'll see that I'm right. I am. The engines work fine – both of them. When the engines shut down, the pilots didn't know to just restart them. If they had, they wouldn't have crashed. They should have just pressed the ignition button again."

Mom just looked at me for a long time and smiled strangely.

"Okay. Okay, I have to call him back anyway," she said.

So she called Dad on his phone, as I listened nearby.

"Jake, listen," she said, "Mack has a theory about the crash, and he's insisting, he's just *insisting* that both the engines work fine, and that if the pilots had known to press restart…"

Then Mom just stared at me silently, as her face lost all its color. She actually looked spooked, even frightened.

She slowly dropped the phone away from her ear and stared at the crystal in my hand again, as though hypnotized. I could hear my Dad's voice shouting through the phone: *"How could he have known that?"* I heard him say, *"How could he have possibly come up with that? Because it's true. That's exactly what happened."*

Chapter Five

Sleepless

I *hate* going to bed early. I don't mean in some spoiled-brat way, like I'm looking for any lame excuse to stay up late. Fact is, I just don't get tired!

"You're like your Dad," my Dad always says.

Isn't it weird when people talk about themselves like it's another person? I mean, why doesn't he just say, "You're like me"? Instead he says, "You're like your Dad." He *is* my Dad! What's he talking about? Mom talks that way too. She'll say, "Drive on icy streets in this weather? Not *this* girl," referring to herself. I don't get it. But I let it slip most of the time and never say a thing.

Anyway, the day after that weird phone call about the plane crash, when I knew what caused it, Dad got back really late from the crash site, and (yup, you guessed it) I was still wide awake. I heard the SUV pull into the driveway to drop him off and I glanced at my clock. One in the morning, and I was still tossing and turning. I punched my pillow and fluffed it up again to make it more comfy, and that's when I heard a *thunk!* My crystal had rolled off the mattress and onto the floor. I found it in the dark with my fingers and put it under my pillow again, and then ordered myself to get to sleep. After a while I could feel it starting to work: my eyes were getting heavy, my breathing was getting slower…

But then I smelled coffee and everything was clear to me.

Dad always liked fresh coffee when he got home, even when it was really late. So, he and Mom probably made some. Here's the thing: I was almost asleep when the smell of coffee sent me to another time, another place. I jumped out of bed and headed downstairs.

Dad probably wouldn't mind me being still awake, but Mom was going to freak out because it was so late. When I was halfway down the stairs, I heard Mom say my name, so I stopped dead still to listen. Wouldn't you?

"I'm telling you, it *frightened* me," my Mom was saying to my Dad in the far room. "And when I looked into Mack's eyes," she continued, "they were, I don't know, in another world. It was scary."

Yup, they were talking about me. Star of the show again.

"I'm sure it was just a lucky guess about the jet engines, Lily," Dad said. "There is no way he could have known that both engines were working," Dad said. "It's imposs – "

Then they both looked up and saw me standing on the stairs.

"Oh my goodness, would you look who's still up," Mom said. "You're in the *wrong* place at this hour, Mack."

Usually I give my Dad a hug when he's been gone for a few days, but I didn't this time. He was just sipping his coffee as I came into the living room and I said, "The coffee… It was the coffee, wasn't it?"

"Oh, so that's why you're up," Mom said. "You smelled coffee and thought it was morning. Go back to bed, honey, it's much too…"

But she stopped talking when she saw the startled look on Dad's face. He's not the kind of guy who loses it, but at that moment he was looking at me wide-eyed with his mouth hanging open.

"It was the coffee, wasn't it?" I asked him again. "In the crash. The pilot spilled his coffee into the wiring and…"

And then – as if he knew what I would say – Dad and I said the same words together at the same time:

"…*it briefly shorted out both jet engines.*"

Dad turned really serious, and pulled me close to him, as Mom looked on silently, a little afraid.

He asked me in a very quiet voice: "Mack, how did you know that? That information wasn't released anywhere. How'd you know that?"

I looked at my Mom before answering. She wasn't exactly reassuring. In fact, she looked at me like I was an alien or something.

I started to speak but my voice started breaking like it does when you're about to cry. I couldn't help it. My folks were flat-out scared.

"I don't know," I said, "It's just a feeling I have, just something I thought of. It's like I *remembered* it, really," I said, a little confused myself.

With that comment, my Mom sucked in a sharp, worried breath. But it didn't scare me, mostly because Dad was still holding me.

"Have you had *other* feelings like this one?" he asked.

"A few," I said.

"When did they starting coming to you?" Dad asked.

"Just since Evers died," I said.

"But how do you get these... these feelings of knowing? Like about the jet engines," my Dad asked.

He was really calm now. And really serious.

"Well, that one came to me when I set up the Legos, you know, after I saw a picture of the crash site."

"Give me that crystal!" Mom blurted out very firmly. She had spotted it in my hand. "Give it to me *now*, Mack. It scares me!"

"No!" I said. "It's mine. He gave it to me. It's a gift!"

"What crystal?" Dad asked, confused. "You mean the rose crystal from Evers' house? Oh come on, that couldn't have anything to do with– "

"*Now,* Mack!" Mom shrieked.

But now *I* was scared, and so was Dad.

So, without another word, I handed it over to Mom. She took it, got up, and marched across the room. I followed her all the way through the kitchen, where she flung open the back door and hurled the crystal out into the pitch-black yard.

Dad didn't exactly rise to my defense, but can you blame him? This was as freaked out as I've *ever* seen Mom, and it was clear that no one was going to mess with her.

We all stood there in the kitchen, not knowing what to do next, just looking awkwardly at each other.

"Look, everybody's tired," Dad said, exasperated.

"I'm not tired," I said. "Well, I *was,* but not anymore."

"Let's just… Let's just go to bed and sort this out in the morning," Dad said.

With that, we all trooped upstairs. I only got to sleep after Mom came in as I was lying in the dark. She stroked my hair and told me everything was going to be okay. It was nice of her, but I didn't think that anything was really wrong.

I woke up early the next morning after I heard Dad get back from his bagel run. He was munching away at the table when I walked into the kitchen.

"Hey kiddo," he said, giving me a friendly wink. I thought that maybe he was pretending that last night didn't happen, or that it might just go away if we didn't talk about it. Fine with me.

I started slicing my bagel as Dad finished his. He was watching me quietly without saying anything. Then he leaned back in his chair with his hands folded behind his head, all casual-like. He was grinning at me in a non-Dad way, like he was chit-chatting with a friend at work.

He finally spoke: "Okay now, 'fess up, buddy. Where are you getting those ideas?"

And then he laughed, half at himself and half at the absurdity of having to ask his twelve-year-old son about air crashes.

"I mean, the most sophisticated crash investigators in the whole country took *two days* to sort this one out. But you… you… Well, you just *knew* what happened."

I laughed a little too, holding out my hands in a helpless "don't ask me!" gesture.

Then we both laughed, and then it suddenly didn't matter how upset Mom was the previous night, because we were both laughing about it now.

"What do you say we go down to Woodbury Toys and get a new Lego project?"

I couldn't believe my ears.

"Battle of Endor?" I suggested, knowing it was $149.99. Took guts to go that big, but why waste a Dad in a good mood?

"Battle of Endor it is," he said without flinching. I knew he was buying me Endor to make up for the whole crystal thing. Hey, who am I to question a loving father's wisdom?

"Go brush your teeth before we go," he said.

I sprinted up the stairs with rockets in my feet. No way Dad could back out of buying me the Endor Lego set now. That set was clearly more the level of a birthday present, or even a Christmas present, and here I was getting it for almost no reason at all.

I dived into bed, looking under my pillow for my wallet, because I had even more money in there. Maybe I could get some Lego accessories too.

But when I slipped my hand under my pillow I felt something hard. Hard like a rock.

I pulled it out, and lo and behold, whether I wanted to believe it or not, there was the rose crystal.

My rose crystal.

The same one that Mom had pitched into the back yard last night.

I hid it in my pocket. I wasn't going to say anything about it until I found out if maybe she had put it back under my pillow. Or maybe Dad put it there, because he knew how special it was to me now. That was it. That's why he winked at me at breakfast. It was an "our little secret" wink.

I made my way into the kitchen again and "casually" asked Dad if he'd been out already that morning.

"Sure, yeah, I went out for bagels," he said.

"Have you maybe been out to *the lawn*, though?" I asked. I think I even winked, so I could turn it into a joke if the conversation went the wrong way.

He looked at me with a perplexed look on his face, his head turned a little sideways.

"The lawn? No," he said. "I couldn't have been. Not on *our* lawn." He went back to reading his newspaper.

"Why not?" I asked, my smile suddenly gone. "Why not *our* lawn?"

"Well, Inspector," he said, "because it's all dirt out there now. The landscapers smoothed it all over so we could plant new grass, remember? And I don't want you going out there either."

I looked outside. Sure enough, the entire backyard was smoothed-over dirt. If anyone had walked on it, you would definitely have seen footprints. Then I looked down at my dad's running shoes. They were clean.

"If you're worried about the crystal," Dad said, "I'm sure we'll find it. I'm sure it's out there, easy enough to find."

"I know where the crystal is, Dad," I said.

"You do?" he said.

I pulled it out of my pocket.

"Mack, did you go out there to get it? This morning?"

"Nope. It was under my pillow this morning. I found it under my pillow."

My Dad's smile faded.

"What?" he said. "How could that be? I didn't get it. And your mother definitely didn't get it...."

He took the crystal and turned it over and over in his hand, mouthing some words I could barely hear. I think what he said was, "Evers? Are you trying to reach us?"

Then he took the crystal and slipped it in his pocket, as if I wouldn't notice. Next he picked up his pen, pretending it was a light saber and that he was in the middle of a duel, saying. "Skywalker lunges! He pivots and jumps! – barely escaping the expert counter-attack from the evil...the evil, uh..."

But he couldn't come up with a single Star Wars name. Pathetic, but hey I just played along anyway. The crystal would come back to me eventually, I knew it.

"The Siths, Dad."

"Ah yes," he said, "the evil Sliths!"

"Not *Sliths,* there's no L in there. It's *Siths!*"

He swung his fake light saber in a wide arc, looking more like a demented Japanese samurai warrior than a Jedi master. And he made the lamest light saber sound that anyone has ever made. Ever.

Chapter Six

The Battle of Endor

When we got back from the toy store, I immediately checked under my pillow, but – you guessed it – no crystal. I figured it only showed up when I didn't expect it. Dad said I had to take a shower before I could assemble Endor, so I went to the bathroom and started the shower, but I actually stayed dressed. Then, with the shower water running full blast to make it sound like I was *in* there – I can like *so fool* my folks whenever I want to – I raced back into my room, hoping to catch someone trying to sneak in. This trick worked last Christmas Eve, when I turned the shower on and – oops, no shampoo – I walked downstairs to the other bathroom, only to catch Mom stuffing the Christmas stockings.

"Just helping Santa out," she said lamely, hiding stuff behind her back. "Because Santa's, um, busy flying around the world in his super sonic sled."

Yeah right.

This time, when I ran back to my room, I froze at the door in case I caught Mom red-handed again. But the room was empty. Had she already been here?

I scanned the room like the *Terminator* cyborg, marking targets with my laser-tag eyes, logging in coordinates for defensive actions.

Wait a minute… Had I put my shirt over my pillow like that? Hmmmm.

Suspicious, but no definitive evidence of an intruder. I tip-toed over to the bed and slipped my hand slowly under my pillow.

Still no crystal.

Back in the bathroom, I stuck my hair under the shower spray for a second to make it look convincing, and turned off the faucets. That's thinking. I had more important things to do than take a shower. Back in my room, I took the plastic wraps off the box holding my latest Lego challenge.

The Battle of Endor Lego set was just about the coolest thing I'd ever seen. It even stood up to the Lego Bullet Train with the extra tracks. Battle of Endor has 950 pieces. Now, sometimes when I'm building, I outsmart the directions to make them simpler. Then, I email the Lego engineers to suggest *much* better ways for sets to be assembled. I think they probably have a folder in a filing cabinet somewhere, nine floors down in an underground toy research lab, that's labeled TOP SECRET: MACK'S MUCH, MUCH BETTER IDEAS.

But for Battle of Endor, they got it just about right, and I didn't need to correct any mistakes. At least for now.

I emailed the Lego engineers a simple four-word message: *Good Job on Endor!!!!* I'm sure that got into my folder too, because even the best engineers in the world need a pat on the back now and then.

With the Endor project done, I needed someone to show it to.

My Dad was in his study, working on his book about the history of famous airplane crashes. Lots of old crashes are still unsolved, especially the ones from before I was born, reaching back to when Dad was a kid. That's because the airplanes back then didn't have black boxes to record the pilots' voices or the flight data just before the crash. Those boxes aren't *really* black, by the way. They're actually a bright orange that makes them easy to find in the wreckage.

"Each crash is a multi-layered mystery," Dad once told me. "A puzzle. I know that people died in these crashes, but we can learn from them to make flying safer."

When I finished my Battle of Endor set, I flew it up to Dad's study.

I can make totally realistic flight sound effects, and I zoomed in with engines and guns blazing. Most people are impressed by my jet engine sounds. But, you see, my Dad's also a pilot, so he knows what jet engines really sound like.

"Wait, don't tell me, let me guess," he said, his hand held up in a "stop" position. I knew he was just playing along, but I appreciated the effort. "F... F ... F9?"

"Nope. Guess again," I said.

"F18?"

"Nope. Give up? It's an AT-AT escort from the Alderon sector."

"Alderon! Gets me every time. Arghhhh," he fake-groaned. "I'm still way behind on my Star Wars sounds."

He could say that again.

"Wow, Mack, that's a wild ship. Can I see the box?" Dad said.

I ran downstairs to get it. I was glad he asked, because I like to show off the fact that the Lego models I build come out *exactly* like they are on the box.

Back in a flash, I handed the box to Dad, and his eyes darted from my model to the picture, back and forth. He was really studying it.

"Amazing, how you can build these things! Just amazing," he said.

"What're *you* working on, Dad?" I asked.

"A crash from 1967. The year your Dad was born," he said.

Again with the "your dad" business. I let it slide this time, to give the guy a break.

"And no one's figured it out in all that time?" I asked, amazed.

"Nope," he said, looking back at his reports and photos.

"But you will," I said.

"I'll try my best. That's all you can do, really. Try your very best, and forget the rest," he said half to himself, as he studied the photos.

"Where was it?"

"Where was what?" he asked, not really paying attention to me anymore. He was busy staring through his magnifying glass.

"The crash, Dad. Where was the crash?"

"Oh. Sorry," he said, looking up. "At an air base in Colorado."

Dad and I looked at the pictures of the crash, and he pointed out the details with the point of his pencil. As he shuffled the photos around, a big pile of papers fell onto his desk.

He picked them up real quickly.

Suspicious.

"Sorry," he said with a guilty look, "Mom asked me to hide it…."

"Hide what?" I asked.

And then I saw it. My rose crystal.

"So *there* it is. You know Dad, that's mine, my personal private property, and …"

I grabbed it really quick before he could stop me, and with that, I immediately stopped talking, because a strange feeling came over me. I suddenly had gotten the idea that my Endor escort fighter needed something more. It didn't feel complete. I had to fix it – *now*. Without a word, I took the crystal and bolted from my Dad's study. He probably thought I was storming away mad, but I wasn't even thinking about my personal property rights anymore. Getting the model just right was all that mattered now.

Back in my room, I rummaged like a boy possessed through my plastic bin of spare Lego parts, looking for … looking for … well, I don't know what exactly I was looking for, but I knew I'd recognize it once I found it.

Ah-ha! I found two more thrusters that were a perfect match, and I added them. I also made the wings longer. Okay, *now* it was finally done. I could just feel it. So, I flew it back up to Dad's study and started to look over the crash scene photos with him again.

Before Dad could say anything, I asked him, "What was the altitude? At the airfield. From that crash?"

"The altitude? Well, I always assumed it was…"

He started shuffling papers, mumbling *"The altitude, the altitude…"*

Then, that same spooky look came over him again – the look he had the other night when I'd told him that the coffee had caused the cargo plane to crash.

He looked at the picture on the Lego box I'd brought up. Then he looked at the rose crystal tucked in my pocket, and then at my Endor escort fighter, the one I'd just modified.

"Mack?" he said.

"What?"

No answer. He just stared at my model.

"*What?*" I said, almost mad that he wasn't speaking faster.

"Son…" he said.

I was like, huh? He never calls me *Son!*

"Where did this ship come from?" he asked, "the new one you have there?" He was pointing to my modified Endor escort fighter.

"It's not pictured on the box we just bought. I've never seen that one before."

"Oh," I said, "I just made it up from extra Lego parts. What's wrong? Why are you so …"

But then I spotted it, the thing that spooked him. It was a crash site photo on his desk. We both leaned in to look together. The center part of the crashed plane was charred, but the wings were intact. And here's the weird part: It had four engines, just like mine *after* I had added the extra thrusters. And the wings were the identical shape of my escort plane, only mine were just a little longer.

"Mack, why did you make your wings that way?" he asked. "Had you seen this photo before?"

"No, why?" I said.

"You sure? I didn't show this photo to you before?" Dad said.

"I've never seen it! Dad, I swear I've never – You and Mom are so, like…"

"Hey, calm down. I believe you," Dad said. "Just tell me this: What did you make the wings longer and add the thrusters? And why did you do that only after you touched the crystal?"

"Well," I said, "the planet Endor has thin very air, even at sea level, even though their seas are made of liquid nitrogen. So I figured I needed more wing length for more lift, since I – "

He cut me off suddenly, saying. "And why the extra thrusters? The same reason? For more lift, because of the thin air?"

Then we both looked at the altitude where the crashed jet was trying to take off: 10,244 feet.

Dad scrambled for more crash records, saying, "If that pilot had been used to flying at sea level, then it wouldn't occur to him that…"

"What? Dad, what are you talking about?" I said.

"Here it is," he said, finally finding what he was looking for. "The pilot in this crash was from Virginia, and this was his first time taking off at high altitude! See, the air is thinner in Colorado Springs."

"*Just like on Endor*," we both said at the same time, and then burst out laughing.

"He didn't give the jet enough thrust," I said, "you know, to accommodate for the thinner air. And so he crashed. Right?"

Dad didn't say anything at first. He just rocked back in his chair excitedly.

"You know," he said with a smile, "maybe I should take you and that rose crystal to work with me sometime."

I almost laughed, before I realized he might just be serious.

Then we heard a strange noise outside. Dad looked out the window and said, "Uh-oh, we've got trouble on the way…?"

"Why, is the evil Sir Harry Dufus Jerkhead lurking around our front door again trying to sell fake magazine subscriptions?"

"No, but I do see Carly out there," Dad said. "And, oh, Mack, give Harry a break. You really could end up friends. Remember, his Dad left him with his Mom, and I don't think he has many friends."

Harry and me, friends? Sure and some day trained sheep will pilot the Space Shuttle. Was he crazy? But I didn't say anything. I kind of just grunted.

"Besides," he went on, looking again out the window, "we have more trouble on our hands than Carly and Harry could ever dish out."

He turned to face me, a sly smile on his face. "It's A.D. in her VW bug."

Chapter Seven

Another Crash

Normally, I am not entirely thrilled to have relatives visit, because, well, let's face it, most of them are as boring as potted plants. And don't even get me started on my Uncle Burt. Watching paint dry is more exciting than hearing him talk about his glory days. Backup high-school quarterback, like so freakin' what!?

But not Aunt A.D.

She has an antique convertible VW bug, cherry red, with a painted-on Band-Aid on the rear bumper where it's dented. She calls it Bugsy, and she almost *always* has the top down. We once drove it with the top down when it was snowing.

"Isn't this great?" she shouted as we drove along with snow piling up in the car. "Who needs a roof anyway?"

That happened when it was like zero degrees outside, and I came home with my jacket soaked, so Mom wasn't too thrilled...even though I think they secretly liked that A.D. was doing something crazy with me. The reason I think that is simple: After that happened, and the news got around, I overheard our neighbor Mrs. Oliver say to my Mom, "What ever happened to the old-fashioned aunts with nice hairdos who used to take their nephews to candy stores for lollipops?"

Mom stuck up for A.D. then. She gave Mrs. Oliver a sweet smile that really wasn't very sweet, if you know what I mean. Then she said, "Oh, you mean the boring, obedient old aunts like I once had? Thank goodness they're facing extinction!"

I ran downstairs from Dad's study as A.D. walked in to the house, and I yelled, "I didn't know you were coming!"

Dad and Mom had come up behind me. They shared a knowing look at A.D. that made me wonder if I were being shipped off to military school.

My Mom just said, "Well, Mack …"

Then she stopped, but her voice made it clear that something had been planned without my knowledge.

Dad said, "We thought you and A.D. could, you know, go for a drive, and maybe sort some things out."

"You know, discuss things," Mom added.

They were all smiling a little too hard. *Something's fishy,* I thought. Then practically at the same time, Mom, Dad and A.D. all said, "You know, talk about the crystal. The crystal. Yeah, the crystal. How you get these ideas from the crystal…"

I shrugged and said, "Fine with me."

"Guess what, A.D.?" Dad said, "Mack just solved another crash."

A.D. and Mom both snapped to attention. "What? When?" they both said in unison.

"It was a baffling crash that happened over thirty years ago, and no one has figured it out. Until now," Dad said, shaking his head in amazement. "It's astonishing to me how--"

"But," Mom said, cutting him off, "he must have done it *without* the crystal, which we've hidden just to give the spirits a little rest. So, you see, it's been a coincidence… "

"Well, actually, Mom," I started to say, but then Dad interrupted me.

"Actually Lil," he said, "I was hidden in my study. Then Mack came in and it essentially fell into his hands, like some force had pushed it off the shelves. Just after he touched it, he immediately ran to his room to build the Lego model that solved the crash."

I pulled the crystal out of my pocket, so Mom could see I had it. All three of them actually backed away a little bit, as if it were radioactive or something.

Then A.D. stepped forward and put her finger to it and pressed it like it was a doorbell to a haunted house.

Mom shivered.

Dad looked mystified.

But A.D. smiled.

"Hey, don't look at me!" I said, turning serious. "I have *no idea* why this is happening. But is it really that bad? Is it really a bad thing that I can predict stuff? Would you rather have another kind of son?"

"Well, Mack, It's just…" Mom struggled to answer the question. "It's just … a little, um…"

She couldn't find the words, but Dad answered by humming Halloween type music.

"Yeah, that's it," she told him.

Then A.D. made them practically jump by shouting, "Road trip!"

"Cool," I said. "Let's go!"

We made for the door, before Mom and Dad could say anything more, and I *couldn't wait* to get out of the house.

But then, as A.D. and I backed out of the driveway, we nearly ran over someone.

"Yikes," she said, hitting the brakes. "Who's that guy, one of your friends?"

"Absolutely not," I said. "It's Sir Harry D.D. The Ds stand for 'dumb-dumb.'"

Then she was actually friendly to him, rolling the window all the way down to say hello, if you can believe it.

"Sorry I didn't see you back there, uh, what's your name?" she said very pleasantly. I guess that was better than taking my word for it and calling him Sir Harry D.D.

"I'm Harry," he said, pretending that he was a nice person. He might fool A.D., but he wasn't fooling me.

"I go to school with Mack," he added with a beaming smile. Then he looked past her and directly at me, and somehow that same smile became a nasty smirk.

"I'm taking Mack out for a ride," A.D. said, but then she said something that really threw me for a loop, given that Harry is my sworn arch-enemy. "Hey, want to come along? It'll be fun!"

I gave A.D. frantic secret hand signals to immediately cease and desist, but she was looking at Harry, not me. What was she thinking?

"Nah," he said. "I've got tons of homework."

Which I knew was a lie. The only homework Sir Dufus ever did was thinking up new ways to torment me.

"Plus," Harry added, "I sold some stuff on eBay today. Some of my dad's stuff. Gotta go pack them up now."

Finally, A.D. drove on, and I said, "I bet anything his Dad doesn't know he's selling that stuff. That's Harry. A real schemer. What were you thinking, inviting him, A.D.? He's… he's the … the enemy!"

"Oh Mack. He's probably just lonely," she said.

"Sure," I scoffed. "Lonely for someone else just as evil as he is. Most of them are not available for play-dates because they're all in maximum security prisons."

Then, as if we weren't already delayed on our trip, A.D. spotted another neighbor of ours.

"That girl looks just like I did when I was her age!" A.D. said.

It was Carly. And I had to admit she *did* look just like a mini-A.D.

As A.D. stopped again, I rolled down the window on my side. "Hey," I called.

"Hi Mack. Whatch'ya doin'?" Carly said.

"Just going for a drive with my Aunt. Maybe to a truck stop. Maybe eat breakfast in the afternoon. Second breakfast for me. I'll eat like four eggs total just today," I said.

"I'm A.D.," A.D. called, reaching out her hand to wave, even though I had never introduced her.

"Oh hi," Carly said, "Oh, A.D.! *The* A.D. Mack's told me a lot about you!"

"I hope the stories are about how I'm a wild woman" A.D. said.

Carly laughed a little nervously.

"Yeah, he *has* told me you're wild," Carly said.

"Oh, he has?" A.D. said, smiling at me. "Well I have a feeling you and me are from the same tribe, Carly. And you know what, we wild women gotta stick together, because … well, have you ever hear of the Bora tribe?"

Carly shook her head no, looking bewildered.

"That's a large tribe of boring people who live secretly amongst us, looking like ordinary civilians, even speaking our language sometimes," A.D said. "Gotta get crazy sometimes and beat back the Bora Tribe. Game?"

Then all of a sudden, Carly's mom called her in, and she skipped off, saying "Bye, Mack. See you later, A.D. Wish I could get tribal with you. The truck stop and all. Maybe next time?"

We finally drove on, making it out of the driveway this time.

"Oh Mack, she's darling! And that Harry doesn't seem so bad. Plus, it's a fact of life that we sometimes have to put up with jerks. If everyone were perfectly nice, how interesting would life be?"

Soon enough, we had Bugsy up to speed and we were on the highway, heading to The Pancake Place. Yes, that's its real name, The Pancake Place. A.D. had heard that I wanted a diner breakfast, even though it was between lunchtime and dinner, and it looked like I would get my wish.

Before long, we were sitting in front of huge plates stacked with silver-dollar pancakes. I tried four different syrups on mine, and the blueberry beat the rest. As we finished, A.D. cleared her throat and said, "We need to talk, because there's something I really need to ask you, Mack."

Nodding, I put my fork down. I just knew what she was going to say, and I dreaded it. She put her hand on the side of her forehead, like she was getting a headache.

"What's the matter?" I asked.

"Oh, I am really in a tough spot here, Mack," she said.

Here it comes, I thought with a sinking feeling, *here it comes…*

"Yeah. I'm not sure if I… if I should… if I should have ice cream on my pie or just have it in a bowl or a sundae."

She winked. And right then I knew she wasn't going to bug me about the crystal. After we finished our ice cream, she even let me play Keno. That's a gambling game you have to be at least eighteen to play, but A.D. let me press the Quick Pick button. When you do that, the machine picks ten numbers for you automatically. After we played ten games, it printed out a ticket to show your numbers.

"Take out the crystal," A.D. said. "Just for fun. Before you pick any more numbers."

I put the crystal on the table and we both pretended to worship it, laughing hysterically.

"All hail the flight crystal," I said, bowing.

After spending ten dollars on Keno, I was just getting going, but A.D. looked at the ticket printout and a startled look came across her face. Suddenly her whole mood changed and she said, "Stop, Mack. Can we stop? Please?"

We finished our desserts, but I felt like we were rushing, and A.D.'s mood had changed. She wasn't mad, but just a little freaked out.

Once we got in the car, she cheered up and was her old self again. But then she *really* got down to business.

"Okay, Mack, tell me, buddy, how do you get these great ideas? These inspirations?"

I shook my head. "I don't know, honest. I just look at the pictures, any photos of the crash scene, and what I build from my extra Legos somehow solves the crash," I said.

A.D. stared curiously at me for the longest time, just trying to figure me out.

When we walked into the house, Dad said in a joking way, "Uh-oh. A.D. has that look on her face, like the time you guys went driving in the snow with the top down."

"Nothing bad!" A.D. laughed, shooting me a warning look that said, *Don't rat us out!*

She was joking. Kind of.

"Just gambling at The Pancake Place with the truckers, *and* having dessert after breakfast. Second breakfast for me," I said. "Four eggs so far for me today."

My Mom and Dad fake moaned, *oh no...*

I drifted off to the TV room, and A.D. asked Mom if she could see the garden, wink wink. I'm sure that was just their excuse to get A.D.'s full report on her conversation with me. I didn't really care, because I was hoping to watch *The Clone Wars* reruns before anyone realized I had the TV on. I was still only allowed to watch two hours of TV a week, if you can even believe it.

The TV room has a window that overlooks the backyard, and I could see Mom and A.D. walking around out there. Is it spying when you just *happen* to be looking out the window to admire the view? Because that's all I was doing.

Yeah, right!

There wasn't much to see – just Mom and A.D. checking out the flowers, so I went back to watching Anakin and Mace Windu battle it out. Then, a sound from the backyard got my attention. It sounded like Mom saying, "What?!" like she was shocked or something. When I went to the window, I saw Dad was outside talking to Mom and A.D. They were all huddled together, looking at something…. the Keno ticket printout, it looked like.

A.D. was shaking her head like she couldn't believe what Dad was saying. But then he ran his finger down the numbers on the ticket right in front of her, and she nodded.

Dad gestured toward the house, and if I could read lips, I swear he was saying *Mack picked these?* over and over again.

Mom just watched, with two fingers pressed against her lips. It was her "worried look," and I knew it well, most recently from when I made a homemade fire extinguisher out of a two-liter plastic bottle, baking soda, and a top-secret formula I'll never reveal until my dying day. Let's just say it involves ketchup and rotten yogurt. Believe me, I knew the *worried look*.

Dad started walking back toward the house, with Mom and A.D. following single-file. It looked very … what's the word, when it looks like trouble is just around the corner? *Ominous* – that's it.

Dad wandered into the TV room, like nothing was wrong, and plopped down on the couch across from me. Mom and A.D. hung out in the doorway, all casual-like.

Then, Dad watched TV with me for a minute without saying anything, like nothing was wrong. But the tension was killing me. They were all pretending to watch too, like *The Clone Wars* was their favorite show. I'd have laughed if I weren't so nervous.

"What?" I finally said, not taking my eyes off Anakin Skywalker.

For about ten seconds, no one said anything. Do you know how long ten seconds can be when you're dying of suspense?

"Mack," my Dad finally said, "how'd you pick those numbers? The Keno numbers."

"Why?" I asked him. "We lost. And besides, the machine picked 'em, I didn't."

"Well, something else interesting came up," Dad said. "You know how I like to study patterns?"

I kept staring at the TV. "Uh-huh."

Then Mom turned the TV off, which was one way to get my attention.

"You know how I like to study patterns?" Dad started in again. "Well, the Keno machine somehow knew our birthdays.

"What?" I said. "Whose birthday?"

Dad showed me the ticket and he ran his finger down the numbers. First, the month and day of my birthday. Then Mom's... Dad's ... A.D.'s...

And finally, and spookiest of all, Evers' birthday!

Then our conversation was cut off by a sound we all knew too well: the crash alert on Dad's Blackberry.

Then the *home phone* rang.

Bad sign. *Must be a big crash,* I thought.

Dad leapt to his feet, ran over to the iMac, and pulled up Google News. He just said, "Oh my God…"

He didn't even stop to explain. He raced upstairs, grabbed his go-bag, pre-packed with his high-tech gear, and raced out the door.

A.D., Mom, and I just watched in astonishment at how fast it all happened.

Within minutes, it seemed, a black SUV pulled up and picked up Dad. I have to admit that those NTSB SUVs were majorly cool. Black and shiny, with black-tinted windows. The dudes who drove them always seemed to wear dark wrap-around sunglasses. And they had earpieces that probably connected them directly to the White House. Man, I wish I could ride in one of those things!

Anyway, whenever the SUVs pulled up, all the neighborhood kids gathered around, just trying to get a glimpse of some of the high-tech gear inside. Today was no different.

As Dad leapt in and the SUV pulled away, I looked down the street and there was "I-got-tons-of-homework" Harry, on his bike, just checking out the latest developments in my life so he could use them against me in school. Doesn't he have a life besides making mine miserable?

When I went back inside, Mom and A.D. and I huddled around the computer to read the news that made Dad rush out of the room. A cargo plane loaded with medical vaccine for yellow-fever had crashed in Miami. You could see photos of it there on the Web, with the plane blocking the highway at the end of the runway.

Amazingly, the pilots survived.

"A miracle," Mom sad. "It's always a miracle when that happens."

But, here's the thing: The vaccine cargo on the plane was headed to Malaysia, where there had been a flood, and if they didn't get it there soon, the news was saying that ten thousand children would die.

There was a second cargo jet – the same make and model of the jet that had just crashed – ready to take off, and it was also loaded with vaccines for the same flooded area. But the NTSB had grounded it until they could figure out what made the first jet crash.

As the night wore on, it got very quiet around our house. Quiet and *weird,* because whenever I went to pick up my Legos, Mom and A.D. got really silent, like … I don't know, like they thought I was going to solve the mystery of the crash or something. To tell the truth, I wasn't much interested in Legos that night. I just wanted to watch some more *Clone Wars* reruns on TV and forget about everything else. So sue me – what do you expect from a twelve-year-old?

Eventually I went upstairs to hang out in my room, because I got tired of hearing Mom and A.D. whispering, like they were plotting a bank robbery or something. Then the phone rang, and I could make out Dad's voice on the speakerphone. I started to sneak downstairs a few times to hear better. But I couldn't get more than a couple steps before Mom would say, "Mack, back upstairs, buddy."

After faking going back upstairs by pounding my feet in place a few times, Mom still somehow knew I was there listening. She yelled, "*Now,* Mack."

Still, I could tell they were still talking about me, because I heard certain words like *Mack* and *Legos* float upstairs now and then. It was a really long phone call with Dad. As I was lying in bed, I heard Mom's, Dad's, and A.D.'s voices raised more than once. They weren't arguing exactly, just trying to talk over each other, until A.D. quieted everyone with a comment that boomed through the whole house: "Why can't we all accept the outrageous fact that Mack is special!? That maybe you should treat his power like a gift and not a curse!"

With those words echoing in my head, I drifted off to sleep.

Before the sun appeared, I woke up to something I would *never* have expected to see in my whole entire life.

Chapter Eight

The Call

It was the sound of a motor outside my bedroom window that woke me up. I looked outside to see one those black SUVs, just like the one that always picked up Dad.

Dad's back already? I wondered.

Suspicious.

But no, turns out Dad wasn't there after all. It was just two of those government guys with wrap-around shades. As I watched, one guy opened the back of the SUV as the other started to load it with … what's that? *Boxes of my Legos?!*

Before I had time to take another breath, I grabbed my crystal. If I ever needed Evers' spirit, it was now.

I dashed downstairs and there was only one dim light on, back in the kitchen. I walked in and Mom was on the speakerphone with Dad, who was still at the crash site. Two very serious-looking men were standing just in the shadows.

It was six in the morning and still dark outside. I could hear Dad's voice over the speakerphone: *"It's our last resort right now, Lily, if we're to get that vaccine over there in time. I mean it, sweetie, this crash has us baffled. Just baffled."*

"I meant what I said, Jake," Mom said. "I'm against this. Dead set against it. Really."

Were they talking about me working on the crash with my Dad? Using *my* Legos?

I stood just out of the light, but Mom must have known I was there.

"Lil," Dad said, *"if there were any alternative to this, I'd… I'd…"* His voice dropped off.

"But it's asking too much of Mack," Mom said. "And you don't know if he even *can* help you, based on … based on what? A couple of lucky guesses?"

"They were *not* lucky guesses," a voice boomed from behind me.

It was A.D.!

She had come up behind me and had been listening all along. She touched my shoulder lightly from behind, and we both stood just outside of the shadows.

But Mom wasn't buying any of this.

"Oh, *come on,* A.D.!" she said in disbelief. "He's a twelve-year-old boy, for the love of God, and you think he can solve the mysteries of an plane crash by touching some crazy rock that his grandfather found in the jungle?"

"Lil, it worked for me," A.D. whispered fiercely.

That stopped the conversation cold. There was a long astonished silence.

Then Mom said, "It? It worked for you? *What* worked for you? What are you talking about?"

"The rose crystal," A.D. sighed, producing what looked at first like my crystal, but slightly different. It was the other half! I had always known there was another part of it, and A.D. had it all along.

"When I was Mack's age," A.D. said, "I used the crystal, too. It couldn't tell the future, not exactly. But it gave me a power to *know* certain things. I don't think it actually *gives* power. It just amplifies certain abilities in the right person. It makes them stronger. Mack is able to use its powers to an even greater extent than I ever could. It's amazing."

"How did it break, A.D.?" I asked her.

She turned and smiled at me. "It was just one larger stone when Evers first got it from that monk in Thailand. Evers said the crystal mysteriously snapped in two, right in his hand, just when Grand-mama died. After that, it sat on a shelf in our sunroom and gave off a wild light. Sometimes you'd walk in there and find a rose-colored rainbow. Yes, the sunroom with the hammock, where you woke up. Some force had brought you there when you were sleeping."

"Jake," Mom asked Dad over the phone, "what's this about?"

"I know it sounds crazy, Lil," Dad said, "but when A.D. was about Mack's age, a piece of the rose crystal gave A.D. some … some power. I thought Evers was just playing a pretend game with A.D. to help her cope with our Mom's death. But then, some things A.D. said would happen did indeed happen. Not only Evers' shipwreck, but his rescue. It was freaky."

A.D. picked up the story: "But then the crystal's power faded, Lil. It seemed inactive and the powers died. Until now. Evers' death freed something, a power for Mack to carry on...."

Mom stared at me and A.D. as though she'd been left out of some ancient secret. And maybe she had.

"Oh Jake. I'm scared," she said to the speakerphone.

"Lil, any other explanation is going to have to wait. Please," Dad said.

Then the two military guys started shifting their feet, and one of them said, "Mrs. McCarthy, we have to go."

Mom hesitated again.

"*Now*, Mrs. McCarthy," the man said, "it's essential that we move immediately." And *his* voice was scary this time. Or maybe it was just the wrap-around shades he wore that gave that impression. It was weird that he was wearing dark shades in the dark, but I figured I'd let him slide on that. For now anyway.

Mom gave me the hardest, longest hug ever, but I was scared out of my wits. I didn't even know what they wanted me to do, or where they wanted me to go.

Then Mom turned to the two military guys and said, "If anything happens to my son, I will personally track you down to the ends of the earth and, well, I don't even want to say what I'll put you through if it ever came to that."

My mouth dropped wide open in amazement.

A.D. pulled me close.

Now the two military dudes wearing tough-guy wrap-around shades looked a little frightened.

"Understood, Mrs. McCarthy, loud and clear, Ma'am," one of them finally said.

"Okay, team, move out," I heard Dad's voice shout over the phone, and then he hung up.

Mom swung into what seemed like *full battle mode*. It was almost scary!

"Do you have the right Legos packed?" she demanded of the military dudes.

"We think so, Ma'am," one of them said.

"You *think* so? *Think?*" she challenged them. They cowered. I wondered if she'd tell them to drop and give her ten pushups. "There are thousands of children's lives at stake here, gentlemen. You'd *better* be sure. Mack," she shouted, making me jump a little bit, "get out to the SUV and do a complete double-check of your Lego inventory. *Move!*"

I moved, all right.

This time she grabbed me on my way out the front door, smiled at me, and whispered, "And kiddo, you've got to get with the lingo, okay?"

We all hustled out to the SUV and one of the military dudes popped open the tailgate. A soft blue light bathed the luggage area. I looked over the Lego supply, which was missing some essential pieces. And then *I* started bossing them around: "Get back in the house – grab my Lego storage box labeled #6. I'll need a full range of thrusters, extra wings for simulations, and all my fuselages."

"Right away sir," they said.

Now, *that* was cool.

"Don't get *too* cocky, kid," A.D. said, smiling in the dawn light that was just starting to show. (That's a line we both knew from the first *Star Wars* movie, in case you didn't know.)

And then I looked deeper into the SUV and – yowza! – it was the most totally cool vehicle you could ever imagine. There were flat-screen TVs on the sides tracking every air flight on earth. And swivel chairs where you could pull up an Internet screen right in front of you while cruising down the highway. And of course, night vision goggles and 3D virtualization helmets for watching simulations. I sat in the chair and punched up the Lego's website, and it came up on screen so fast, I couldn't believe it.

We loaded up the last boxes just as the neighborhood kids started on their way to school. I looked up and – oh, what do we have here? – little ol' Harry on his kiddy bike, watching everything from the edge of the circle of activity. The way his mouth was hanging open, I should have said, "Trying to catch flies, Sir Dufus?" He was obviously dying to know what was

going on. He even tried to get my attention by waving at me —
something he *never* did before. But I ignored him while I
strapped on some night vision goggles, even though the sun was
starting to come up and I didn't really need them. Still, when I
looked at Harry, he was all green and spooky, like an alien. I
took the goggles off just as another alien pulled up on another
bike. It was Carly.

"Hi, Carly," I said, but someone else said it at the exact
same time. It was A.D., and Carly walked over to talk to her. I
went back to what I was doing, because, well, I realized that
saving children was a lot more important than impressing her.

We loaded up the last boxes, and I leapt inside the SUV,
and the doors closed.

Then I realized I didn't know where we were going.

"Pardon me, but, uh, where are we actually going?" I
asked the military dude driver.

"Crash Site: Miami," he said. "We have an NTSB Go-
Team jet waiting for us at a private airfield just six clicks north
of here.

"Six clicks, huh?" I asked, not really sure how far a click
was. "Any chance we could stop for pancakes?"

I wish I could say I was joking, but pancakes really
would have been the perfect finish to the Proudest Moment of
My Life.

Very seriously, the driver looked at me in the rear-view mirror and said, "Negative on stopping for pancakes, sir. They're already waiting for you on the jet."

Chapter Nine

The Crash Scene

All the excitement of flying on a private jet wore off when we pulled up to the crash site. My Dad had seen lots of these scenes before, but not me. The wreckage was astounding to see. And the smell! Fumes from the jet fuel filled the air and crawled up my nose. Fire trucks had put out most of the fires, but a few trucks still stood by, all tangled up in hoses, in case anything started burning again.

"Mack!" my Dad shouted when the SUV dropped me off. "I'm so glad to see you. How about that jet plane you came down in? You've always wanted a ride in that, huh?"

But I couldn't really speak. I looked over the crash scene again and was barely able to keep from crying.

Dad didn't notice how upset I was at first.

"We'll call Mom and A.D. and let them know you're here and..." he said.

"I can't believe the wreckage, Dad," I said. "Are you sure, *absolutely sure* that no one ... you know, died?"

"Mack, no one died here. Both pilots are fine. In fact, you're going to meet in a few minutes."

"No one on the ground was hurt? I mean, look how wide the path of the fire was!"

"Mack, listen to me," he said, a little fed up that I kept asking, "*No one was hurt.* Now, look, we have a lot at stake here. We have another Airbus 230 Cargo over there" – he pointed to the runway behind us – "and it's grounded until we get this figured out."

Then, in a kind of whisper, like he was embarrassed, he said, "You do have the crystal, right? You remembered to bring it?"

I nodded.

Behind us, two very official-looking men in black jumpsuits stood holding my Lego boxes. Dad nodded to one of them and said, "Rob, get those Legos set up in the situation room, and have the pilots ready to meet Mack in an hour."

"Yes sir. Right on it," one of the men said.

Dad put in a quick call to Mom and A.D. to let them know that I was safe.

Then we walked around the area of the crash site. Dad explained what little he and the other NTSB investigators knew about the crash.

"It's an Airbus 230. A very safe plane, normally. The black box data recorder showed that they got good lift coming off the runway, but then the plane dropped like a stone from an altitude of three hundred feet. If it were any higher, the pilots would have been killed on impact."

It was especially scary to walk up close to the wreckage of the plane.

Dad's phone rang. He answered it, and listened without saying anything. He finally sighed like something was a huge nuisance and said, "Okay, right. Bring it over."

With that, one of the military dudes who picked me up that morning raced over with a Scott Pak. That's the thing the firemen have with the yellow tanks. He showed me how to use the pressure regulator, then carefully fit the face mask over my head so I wouldn't smell the fumes.

Dad said in a low voice, "Is all this necessary, Lieutenant?"

The military dude said, "Yes sir, the boy's mom and aunt called to make sure he wasn't in danger of inhaling any fumes, so I immediately requisitioned this Scotty, as I have discerned in my past dealings with them that this was a direct order from the top."

Great, I thought with a frown. Did they ask him to make sure my shoelaces were tied, too?

"Thank you, Lieutenant," I said, though with the face mask on, it sounded more like *"Tahngyuroodenen."*

Then another of the military guys who picked me up said that he had two additional requests. "First," he said, "could you please eat these carrots sometime between now and lunch," he said, handing over a bag. "Your Mom's orders. And second, please text your Mom *and* your aunt and tell them I've done absolutely everything they asked, so maybe they'll quit…. Well, can you just do it, *please?*"

"Ooofffffccccrrrssse," I said through the mask, which I planned on taking off as soon as we got inside.

"Okay," Dad said, smiling, "let's go meet the pilots and maybe have a go at those Legos. No pressure," he added, nodding towards the second Airbus 230 Cargo that was being loaded with vaccine. "No pressure at all…"

In the Situation Room, the two pilots sat drinking coffee, dressed in blue jumpsuits. They told me their names were Carl and Peter. It felt strange calling men almost as old as Evers by their first names.

I let them do the talking, and Carl started by explaining a series of events that were really very simple. Their takeoff was normal and they had good thrust from the engines. Then the plane just nose-dived and crashed.

"It was almost like a strange force made the plane go down," said Peter.

When he said that, Dad caught my eye as if to say, "taking notes?"

Carl nodded, and said, "Even though I was pushing it to full thrust, we couldn't overcome the downward force of the plane," he said. "I've flown tens of thousands of hours in jets around the world, and I've never experienced anything like it. Never."

Peter looked on, nodding. Both pilots were mystified.

I pulled Dad aside and said: "Do these guys know anything about the… you know the…?"

"The crystal?" my Dad whispered back. "Oh no… no. That's secret."

Then he spoke to the whole room. "Okay, let's break for chow and see what we can come up with. I have one more NTSB team doing a last sweep of the crash, and we'll look at all the evidence as soon as we can."

Then Dad led me into a quiet, cool room where all my Legos were in neat piles on a big stainless steel table. One wall had a very big mirror that looked kind of dark. I put my Scott pak mask back on and checked it out in the mirror. Cool! As I did, I swear I saw something or someone move behind it. Was that a two-way mirror, where people could see me and I couldn't see them?

"You okay alone here for a while, Mack?" my Dad asked me. "I'm going run out and get some coffee. You tinker with those Legos and see if you come up with anything. Oh, and there's a picture of the jet on the wall, if that helps. Now, I'm going to be in the next room taking a break, but I'll be able to watch you the whole time."

Dad pointed to the dark mirror. I *knew* it! A two-way mirror! Just like in the movies.

"If you need anything, just wave and I'll come right in, okay?"

"No pressure, Dad," I said, half smiling. "No pressure at all."

He left, and the place got real quiet, but from the next room I heard the voice of a man who said, almost shouting, *"Jake, this is the craziest thing I've ever done. But if it worked for you before, it's worth a try."*

They were obviously talking about me.

I held the crystal as tight as I could. I mean, I really gripped it and squeezed. Then I put it back in my pocket and started to build Legos. Working from Dad's picture, I made a model of a plane that looked sort of like the Airbus 230. But I just didn't *feel* anything. Now that I thought about it, I don't think I felt anything special those other times when I *did* get my super-inspiration. I mean, there wasn't a powerful *zap!* or weird music or sound effects like there'd be in the movies. I must have worked there at the table for about an hour. I built some houses, and a runway, but then screw it, I started working on some Star Wars stuff instead. Then, I suddenly felt sleepy. You'd be tired too if you had been up before dawn like I had. I lay down on a couch in the corner, just to relax a bit. That was the last thing I remembered before I fell quickly and deeply asleep.

I woke briefly to the sound of a raised voice from nearby, saying *"I knew this was a god-damned waste of time. The kid hasn't come up with anything."*

As I looked around the room, official looking dudes had flooded in and they were all standing around the table where I'd been working, looking doubtfully at my pile of Legos. One guy picked up one of my custom Star Wars attack ships and held it up like he was holding a rat by its tail, turning it from side to side and looking bewildered. At that moment, I felt worse for my Dad than for the thousands of kids who needed the vaccine that was waiting on the runway, waiting for *me* to figure out why the first plane had nose-dived.

I buried my head in a pillow and tried to go back to sleep.

Chapter Ten

Let Down

The next time I woke up, it was to the sound of my Dad's voice, talking to Mom on the phone. He was half-sitting, half-leaning on the armrest of the couch where I'd been dozing.

"He's waking up now, Lil," he said. "Yeah, I'll be sure to have him call you in a few. Sure thing. Yup."

He paused a moment while Mom said something. Then Dad said, "I know, I know, it was all just too much to put on Mack, and I think he just got overwhelmed. Yup, Yup. Okay, we'll talk about that when I get home. Okay, Lil. Bye for now."

Then Dad turned to me, as I looked around and noticed that the room was cleared of all the Legos. It was really kind of a relief for me. A *big* relief.

"You really zonked out there, Mack," he said. "You slept for a couple hours."

"Did the second plane get to take off?" I asked. "Did you solve it? Did you solve the crash?"

"See for yourself," he said, and signaled me to follow him to the window.

I did, and we both looked out to see the second Airbus 230 Cargo jet swing around at the end of the runway, and then start its take-off. We watched without saying a word as it reached high up into the sky, and finally moved out of sight.

"So what was it?" I asked. "What made the first jet crash?"

"Cargo shift," my Dad said. "Whoever loaded the jet didn't secure a cargo container. And since the cargo pallets are on rollers, they shifted, throwing all the cargo weight to the front of the plane. With that much weight rushing forward of the wings so fast, the pilots didn't have a chance to respond, and the plane nose-dived. One member of our crash investigation crew found the broken cargo straps on their last sweep through the wreckage."

I nodded. "Not something I could have solved with Legos anyway, huh?"

"Mack, I put too much pressure on you, flying you down here to help us solve that crash. You're so smart, I sometimes forget that you're still a kid."

"Well," I said, trying to think of something positive to say to make him feel better, "the SUV was cool."

"Isn't it? Coolest ride in the world!"

"And the private jet was even cooler."

"Well, we're flying home in that jet today, so the fun isn't over yet," he said.

"Awesome. Where are my Legos?" I asked.

"They all got loaded into the jet already, Mack."

"I guess the crystal doesn't really work after all, does it?" I said.

Dad just gave me this look that seemed to say, *Oh, well, it was a nice fantasy while it lasted.*

"But what about that stuff A.D. said?" I asked. "And the part about how she helped Evers with the crystal? Was that just a coincidence?"

"Well, sometimes we want something to be true *so* much…" he said, and then he paused to search for the right words. "Some things may seem true," Dad said, "even though they aren't. So we force-fit our version of reality over what's actually real. Eventually the truth comes out."

Deep down, I knew that he was talking about the crystal almost as much as he was talking about his own belief that I could help solve the crash.

"Maybe I should leave it here," I said. "The crystal, I mean. You know, just plant it in the dirt and let it grow in someone else's imagination,"

"See," Dad said, ruffling my hair, "it's times you say things like that I think you're wise beyond your years--an Old Soul, as A.D. would say. But let's take the crystal home. It may not be powerful, but it's a pretty and it *was* a gift from Evers. Plus it's half of a matched set, and A.D. has the other one."

We packed up the last of our stuff and headed out to the runway, not before I checked out a pretty cool garden they had there. It had memorial stones for a couple of pilots who must have died years ago at the airport. Now, *this* would be a good place to leave the crystal, I thought.

The jet to take us home was just a few feet away, idling with a high-pitched whine. When we got on board, Dad knocked on the cockpit door. It opened and Dad chatted a bit with the two pilots inside.

"Short hop today," Dad told them, as everyone smiled.

"Just another milk run," one pilot said.

As we buckled up in our seats, I asked Dad, "Are they shipping milk someplace?"

He kind of laughed, then told me, "Oh no, that expression just means this will be an easy flight, like running for milk to the corner store."

We taxied down the runway, but I didn't even look out the window. That's because all these NTSB government jets that Dad flies have *fantastic* Internet connections, with big screens and noise-canceling headphones. In no time, I was deep into a Star Wars game, blasting away with Anakin while we saved the universe once more from an unimaginable range of dire threats.

Dad was dozing off in the seat across from me. I really, really hoped he wouldn't lose his job or anything because of me. Maybe his co-workers even thought he was a fool for thinking I had mystical powers of some kind.

It was kind of boring with no one to talk to, so I started playing with – you guessed it – my Legos. Most of our luggage and stuff was in the cargo section, but a couple of my Lego boxes were up front with me. So I broke out a few pieces and started to assemble a jet that turned out to look a lot like the one we were flying in. Since I had time to kill, with Dad snoring away, I really made it elaborate, with plastic Lego rods controlling the wings and actual working gears that linked to the tail. I added landing gear too that could fold up into the belly of the plane. I have to say it was one of my most excellent creations. I was flying it around by hand, trying out some new jet noises, when it suddenly got tangled in something.

Was that a rope hanging down?

But it wasn't a rope. I was a clear hose of some sort, and at the end of it was a facemask.

I looked up...and gulped in fear. It was the oxygen mask above my seat! I didn't push the button for it to release. It only drops down on its own when there's a loss of air pressure inside the jet.

Dad's mask had dropped too.

I woke him up, shaking his shoulder. "Dad... Dad!"

"Wha--?" he said groggily. "Darn it, Mack, how many times have I told you not to...?"

I didn't answer. I just pointed to our face masks swinging in the air. That sure woke him up in a hurry.

"When did – ?"

"Just now," I said.

It was then that we heard a terrible mechanical grinding sound. It was like a car crash, but the screeching was non-stop, and deafening.

"Get back in your seat, now," he said. "Buckle up."

I tried to, but my hands were shaking like crazy. "Dad, I'm scared!" I said.

Normally this was when he would laugh and say something reassuring like, "Don't worry, it's just a normal sound the plane makes."

But he didn't.

He said, "Me too, Mack." Then I was double-scared.

Dad bolted up from his seat to talk to the pilots. But just as he stepped in the aisle, the jet took a nose drive, throwing him forward against the front wall of the plane.

I screamed, "Dad!" but he couldn't hear me.

The cockpit door opened, as the pilots fought to level the plane.

"Jeez, Jake. This plane's going crazy!" one of the pilots shouted over the grinding sound.

"Disconnect the autopilot," my Dad screamed. "Go to manual flight."

"We already did," the captain screamed back. "I can't figure what the heck is going on!"

The plane leveled a bit, but then it rolled to the right, so we were all leaning way over to one side.

My Dad had tumbled backwards, but he fought to get back to the cockpit door.

Then he turned to the pilots and said, "Can you override the electronics and fly manually?"

"Working on it," the co-pilot said.

Then I heard the radio call the pilot made from the cockpit. It was a radio call whose words I'd read in so many black box voice recordings.

"Mayday, mayday," he said. "This is flight Oscar Niner Hotel. Mayday. We have eighty-five percent loss of flight controls. Passing rapidly down through twenty thousand feet. Repeat: Mayday. Approaching complete loss of aircraft control."

An air traffic controller's voice came over the radio: "We read you, sir, O-9-H. Souls on board?"

"Four souls on board, sir. Four," the pilot yelled over the grinding noise, which seemed to get worse by the minute. "We'll try to set down in an unpopulated area," the pilot said.

"Okay, keep us updated on status. We are here to assist," the air traffic controller said.

I really started to panic then. I didn't much like how the pilot and air traffic controller called us "souls." No one calls people souls unless they're *dead*.

I looked at my Lego plane, the one I had just made that looked just like the jet we were flying. Don't ask me how I happened to notice it just then, but one of the hydraulic rods that controlled the wings on my model was missing. I could barely sit up enough to think straight, but I yelled out: "The hydraulics! It's the hydraulics!"

My Dad spun around to look at me in confusion, looking first at me, and then at the Lego model. I pointed to the access panel on the floor, and his face seemed to say: *Of course!*

The plane rolled to the other side, throwing Dad against the wall. He fought back, and pried open the floor panel with the claw end of a hammer he'd grabbed out of the emergency tool kit on the wall. There wasn't a whole lot I could see while being buckled in my seat, but Dad's hand were immediately covered in hydraulic oil. It looked like brown blood.

"Found the problem," he yelled to the pilots. "Blown hydraulics." He looked around a little helplessly as he said, "Now, how to patch this damn thing?"

Then he shouted to me, "Mack! Get me that tool kit from behind my seat. See if there's a hydraulic clamp in there. It'll be marked H-22."

I unbuckled my seatbelt, and tossed my Lego aside, which brought into hundreds of pieces. I hoped *that* wasn't a prediction and how our jet would break. Then I crawled along the floor to where Dad was opened the tool kit, but *what the--?* It was just bandages and iodine and...

"No, that's the first aid kit. The other box, Mack. The blue one!"

The jet rolled again. We were barely holding on.

I grabbed the right box and found the clamp and tossed it to Dad. He caught it and cinched it into place, but it didn't stop the oil. It just slowed it, by about half.

"Got it," he yelled. "Not perfect. But I got it."

The pilots fought the jet back to a level position. It was wobbly, but at least we were flying.

They radioed to the air traffic controller again. "This is Flight Oscar Niner Hotel. We have regained sufficient control to land. Please direct us to the nearest air field. We are a fire hazard. Repeat, we are a high-risk fire hazard, with leaking fluid."

I was scared nearly out of my wits until I saw Dad buckle up for landing. And I *know* he didn't believe it when he looked at me and said: "It'll be a piece of cake now, Mack. Piece of cake."

I knew he was just trying to calm me down. If landing was going to be such a *piece of cake*, why did Dad make me assume the crash position with head between my knees?

Instead of a smooth landing, we *slammed* down, hitting the runway with a thump, followed by a quick high bounce, and then we rolled to the end of the runway. If you ever wanted to see a *great* selection of fire trucks, and you don't have to wait for the 4th of July parade, all you had to do was look out the window as we landed, because they were all lined up to welcome us.

Before we were even fully stopped, the door sprang open and a fireman in a metallic-silver protective suit and silver hood sprayed foam all around the doorway. Dad swung me off my feet, and practically threw me out of the plane and into the hands of an Emergency Medical Technician. I looked back as he pushed the pilot and co-pilot out of the plane, and then he leaped into the foam and starting running…

… just as the plane burst into a HUGE fireball.

When we turned back to look at it, feeling the heat of the burning jet from over a hundred yards away, that's when I *really* got scared. I couldn't believe we were all somehow spared.

"We're four souls indeed. Lucky souls," one of the pilots said.

I nodded, thinking, *Yes, we are.*

Chapter Eleven

Last Flight Home

The next time I saw a jet door swing open, it was on a commercial jet, and it was at our home airport. Mom and A.D. rushed up, as Dad and I walked down the ramp, and Mom hugged me so hard that I could hardly breathe. I eventually had to say, "Great, I survived a plane explosion, only to be squeezed to death."

I mean, jeez!

But just as soon as Mom let go of me, A.D. did the same thing. I swear I heard one of my ribs break, but it was just a carrot in my backpack.

As soon as we got home and piled out of the SUV, a couple very serious-looking dudes in dark glasses seemed to appear out of nowhere to carry our stuff into the house. We didn't have much. All my Legos were burned in the crash. You might think I was really upset over that. I wasn't. First of all, it wasn't my whole collection. Second of all, hel-lo? …can you say major Lego shopping spree to replenish my sets?

As I looked around, wow, now there was a *real* gathering of kids around our driveway. I had to admit it was pretty cool that they were there, even though I pretended not to really notice them. Oh sure, Carly and Harry were there, but tons of other kids I hardly even knew were there too. They huddled around in semi-circle, with some circling on their bikes, swooping in to try to get a glimpse of what was in the SUV. Everyone once in a while, one of the dudes in dark glasses shot them a scary look that clearly said, *Back off.*

As we made our way to the house, Mom walked over to the kids and told them that I'd had *way* too much excitement for one day, and that they'd have to catch up with me after I get some rest. I was just glad she didn't add "and after I tuck him in…"

There were still a few grumbles. That stopped when A.D. came out with two boxes of Klondike bars and handed them out to everyone.

Then we all went inside and flaked out on the couches. I tinkered with my Legos, and Dad told the whole story to Mom and A.D., starting with the landing.

"Wait, start at the beginning, in Miami at the crash site," Mom said, and then Dad went through the whole story of how I tried and tried to build Legos to solve the mystery of why the first cargo plane crashed, but that the NTSB guys finally figured it out. And how the small jet we flew home had a bad hydraulic line, and how we didn't even know anything was wrong until my oxygen mask got tangled up in my Lego. And how we had to rip open the floor and improvise a clamp that gave us just enough power to land.

"It sounds like you were in a movie," Mom said.

"Yeah, except it wasn't nearly as much fun," I said.

"But Jake, how did you know what was wrong, and how to fix it?" A.D. asked.

Dad just gestured with a sly smile, pointing at me. And I just smirked and held up the Legos I was working on and said, "Lucky guess?"

"The crystal," Mom whispered, and A.D. looked on hopefully and asked me, "Where is it now?

Dad jumped in and said, "Oh, I'm sure he's got it in his…"

"It's in the garden," I said.

"The garden? What garden?" Dad said as he shot a look out the window, thinking that maybe I put it out there when I got home.

"No Dad," I said, "the memorial garden at the airport in Miami, remember?"

Mom and Dad just stared at me in amazement, like I had a purple carrot growing out of my forehead.

"Do you mean to tell me," Dad said, "that you didn't have it with you on the flight home? When you solved the crash?"

"Nope," I said, "I told you I was going to plant it so it could grow--"

"*--in someone else's imagination,*" Dad and I said at the same time.

Mom's eyes darted to everyone else's eyes around the room. "You...you mean," she stammered, "you mean that you solved the last crash..."

It was actually an almost crash, but I didn't say anything. Figured I'd let it slide for now.

"You solved that *without* the crystal?" A.D. said finishing Mom's sentence.

I looked just at A.D. and she winked.

Mom looked really relieved for some reason.

That's when I noticed A.D.'s backpack packed by the back door. Was she leaving? And why had she packed a backpack and not her suitcase?

"What, are you going camping?" I asked, changing the subject.

"Kinda," A.D. said. "Even before this latest adventure of yours, I decided I was going to make a shrine for Evers, with my half of the crystal. I was actually hesitating about leaving it behind somewhere, because I thought it might deprive someone, namely you, of a power to do some good. But maybe you don't even need it after all?"

"Where're you going? And why aren't you bringing a suitcase?" I asked, a little worried.

"Thailand. " A.D. said, "I'm going back to the place where Evers first got the crystal, and I'm going to make a shrine for him there."

"Well, can I... can I go?" I said, half demanding that I come with her.

"Oh no, Mack, not on this trip," my Dad said. "This is one that A.D. has to do by herself."

My Mom looked on and nodded firmly, with a look that I knew also meant "*End of discussion.*"

"When are you going?" I sighed.

"Well, I already missed the flight I was supposed to be on, but now that you're both safe and sound, I'm going to leave tonight," she said.

I don't know why, but I had a bad feeling about A.D.'s trip. Maybe it was because she was leaving so quickly after Dad and I were almost killed, or maybe I just felt sad she wouldn't be around.

It all seemed to happen too fast. I mean, the kids outside had barely finished their Klondike bars, and already A.D. was saying her goodbyes and giving me a big goodbye hug. I didn't want to leave her alone for some reason; I thought I had to protect her in some way, and there was a lump in my throat. Just before she closed the door, she said in a low voice so just I could hear it: "You've got the power now. It's all yours. Mack, I'm changing planes in Narita, Japan at around 3 A.M. your time, and I'll think especially of you when I step off the plane, knowing you're safe in your bed."

And with that she was gone.

I thought it was strange that she'd tell me what time she was changing planes. In fact, right after she said it, she got a funny look – like she wondered why she'd even said that to me.

As she drove off to the airport, she spotted Carly in our yard. I could just see them through the window. A.D. called Carly over, and I could see that A.D. took off one of her necklaces and gave it to Carly, who looked very surprised. Even though I couldn't hear them, I could tell Carly was saying, *"Wow, thanks, Wow thanks!"*

She put it on and wore it over her shirt, and after A.D. drove away, Carly skipped home, so you could tell she thought it was pretty cool.

That night, Mom sat on the edge of my bed and talked to me just as I was going to sleep. She told me that I was going to be hot stuff at school for a while, because of the "almost" plane crash. But she said that I had to be careful not to get carried away, because the kids would eventually forget all about it and I'd go back to being just plain old Mack in their eyes.

"Some people may be resentful of all the attention you're getting and find some way to try to tear you down," she said.

"That would be Harry," I quickly interjected.

"But you know what?" Mom said. "I've found that people like Harry *secretly admire* the person they are trying to knock down a notch or two. They actually wish they were that person. Sweetie, this is a good lesson for you for something we've talked about before. You can't tie your sense of who you are to what other people think. It's got to come from inside."

Then she quoted a poem called "If" by some guy named Kipling that she said she'd learned in high school, and it went like this: *"If you can meet with triumph and disaster and treat those two impostors just the same; yours is the earth and everything that's in it."*

I didn't really understand it at first. After all, what did it mean for *triumph* to be an *imposter?* But the more I thought about it, I figured she was saying that I should be who I am no matter what happened to me. Thing is, I wasn't sure I knew who I was, and I just drifted off to sleep hoping that A.D. was safe as she flew across the ocean.

I don't even know how long I was asleep, but I bolted awake with a chill going down my spine.

Weird!

I looked around my room and a beam of moonlight was shining right on my Lego airplane collection, and the clock showed exactly 3 A.M.

Chapter Twelve

School Stories

I admit it. I *loved* going to school my first day back after our plane nearly crashed. I mean, really, how often does anyone keep a plane from crashing, especially one with you on it? Everyone wanted me tell the story of the crash over and over again. It was like I had become a famous teacher, because my teachers gathered around *me* to hear what happened. Even Harry was silent as he listened. Carly was there too, of course, looking very cool with the necklace A.D. gave her. She chimed in every now and then to confirm things I'd said, like when I told them about being inside the SUV with all the high-tech gadgets. "It was *amazing*," Carly said, shaking her head up and down, "I only saw it from standing outside, of course, when the two armed men opened the tailgate to load Mack's Legos for him. They were like servants. Oh and did I mention they were armed?"

"I could have carried the Legos myself," I said modestly, "but when the government sends top agents to do the job, then, well…"

"Oh you should have seen Mack's Mom ordering those guys around!" Carly said. "And because it was still dark when they were packing up, Mack got to put on these very cool--"

"Night-vision goggles," a voice said, but it wasn't Carly. It was Harry! "Those were so totally awesome!"

I couldn't believe it. Harry was actually *not making fun of me*. I looked up at Harry and I think I even smiled at him. Carly did too.

Dad was at home in his study when I got home from school. He was taking some time away from the office to study the jet we almost crashed in.

"How was school?" he asked me as I ran by to the kitchen.

"Ridiculously magnificent," I said, and I wasn't kidding. I grabbed an apple and went out on my bike. Harry was there with his bike, and he asked if I wanted to bike over to Carly's and see if she could come out. Wow, I guess it takes almost dying to make new friends. I was so stunned that I just said, "Yeah, okay" without even remembering Harry was my worst enemy. We went to Carly's and she was there, and we all hung out, playing Risk. As I started to pack up to leave, Harry got kind of weird and announced that he had something to show us. I figured that he'd try to do something to make himself look big now, and I was right.

"What I am about to show you, actually *to give to you,* can't be known nor seen by parents," Harry said, sounding almost like an international spy. Or a lawyer – I wasn't sure which. "Deal?" he said.

"Deal," Carly and I said at the same time.

Then Harry leaned in and grabbed my shirt, and bunched up the front of it to pull me closer to his face. I thought he was going to hit me, and he said, "Never, *ever,* okay?"

"Never, ever," I said.

"Jeez, Harry," Carly said, "lay off. What have you got, a portable nuclear bomb or something?"

Harry gave us a "wait a minute" signal with his finger, then reached into his backpack and grabbed something wrapped in a T-shirt. He pulled out three gleaming iPhones, and handed one each to me and to Carly.

"Wow, cool," I said. "But are they connected to the Internet?"

"Yeah, Harry, can we make calls?" Carly said.

"That's the part you can't tell anyone about," Harry said. "You see, let's just say that my Dad ... Well, let's just say that he doesn't always play on the right side of the law, if you know what I mean."

Suddenly, Carly was wide-eyed and holding the phone like it was a dead rat, but I just listened, pretending not to be all that impressed.

"He had these iPhones turned on by a guy in New York City," Harry explained. "And they're completely untraceable. They're programmed for unlimited free use and the bill goes to some big company out in Utah. Look, my dad even got me one of their credit cards! They'll never notice!" Harry said, holding up a shiny new Visa card.

"See," he went on, "I can even get on eBay and sell stuff, *right from the phone*. Plus, I have all three of these iPhones pre-configured so we can Instant Message each other on Sykpe. Try it!" Harry said, just thrilled to be sharing his secret.

I logged in to Skype IM and Harry and Carly did too, and we synced up. The things worked, just as Harry said they would.

Carly was really quiet. Obviously she was thinking the same thing I was, that Harry's "gifts" didn't seem to be on the level. But I only pretended to be worried. Sue me, but I couldn't wait to get home with my new iPhone to try out some apps. As I walked back home, I hid my phone, switching it to vibrate instead of ring as I wandered up to my Dad's study.

"What're you working on now?" I asked Dad.

He had his reading glasses on and was concentrating on a webpage that was filled with numbers.

"Well, Mack, I'm working on something that I hesitate to even tell you about," he said.

"Why?" I asked.

"Because," he said, "it's a story about how people value money over people's safety, and it steams me just thinking about it."

"What do you mean?" I asked.

Dad pointed to the webpage he was reading. He indicated a series of numbers on a chart as he explained: "There's a jet that was in service several years ago with an American airline. A 747. But you know what it means when someone says something is a 'lemon'?"

"Yup," I said, "that's when something is so screwed up at the factory that it can't be fixed. Ever." I saw it on Discovery Channel.

"Exactly," Dad said. "Well, this 747 *was* a lemon. *Is* a lemon, I should say. It has a history of losing altitude suddenly."

"Why didn't you guys take it out of service?" I asked.

"Well, the airline *did* take it out of service, but somehow the plane ended up getting sold in the international charter plane black market. We last lost track of it in Thailand. The new owner tried to change all its identifying tags, starting with the tail fin tag. Thing is, these gangster idiots don't really know that there's *lots* of ways to identify a plane. The original serial number is actually written in lots of places, not just on the tail fin. You can see it on the door tags, or even etched in the window frames. We just got a bunch of global alerts out on this thing, and we're working with the FAA in trying to figure out where the 747 ended up."

"Weird," I said. "It's a huge airplane and no one knows where it is?"

"I know it seems unlikely that a 747 could get lost, but it did, and it's flying around somewhere right now. The real problem is that the pilots and crew have no idea what trouble they're in potentially. And of course the passengers wouldn't know either. The NTSB believes that the 747 has a high probability of crashing on its next trans-oceanic flight."

"You said something about the charter plane market?" I said.

"Yeah," he said, and started to explain, "that's when a private company buys a plane and – "

"Oh, I know what it is, because A.D. told me all about it. That's what she's flying home from Thailand," I said.

"*What?*" Dad asked, looking up suddenly and very surprised. "How do you know that? We dropped her off at the regular terminal. She's flying a regular commercial airliner, not a charter."

"She changed that. She's taking a commercial jet over because she missed his first flight waiting for me and you to get home," I said. "But she's taking a charter flight home. Said it was cheaper. She told Carly all about how she got a cheap ticket online."

That's when Dad started getting a little frantic. "When did all of this happen, Mack? When did she tell Carly this?"

"Just before she left," I said.

Dad leapt for his phone. He hit speed dial and someone picked up instantly. He had the phone on speaker and I heard everything.

"Becky, it's Jake," my Dad said. "Can you put an NTSB trace for a week from Monday, the twelfth, on charters flying out of Thailand, and connecting through …" Dad couldn't think of her connecting flight, so he pointed at me.

"Um, Nuruti or something," I said.

Dad gave me a puzzled look. "Nuruti? Do you mean Narita. Narita, Japan?"

"Narita, that's it!" I said.

"Connecting though Narita, Japan," Dad said into the phone. "And if you find a match, can you pull the serial numbers off the plane's record and send those to me as well? You can ignore the tail number because they probably painted over that. Only the serial number, okay? I have to cross-reference them to see if there's a bad 747 in the mix here."

The voice on the phone said she'd get back to Dad as soon as she had anything.

"Becky, I gotta ask a favor here," Dad said, "as a friend…"

"*Anything, Jake, what?*" the voice said.

"My sister could be on that plane – the black market 747 we've been looking for. Can you really push this search through fast?" Dad said, his voice cracking a little bit. He was worried.

Then Dad jumped from his chair and dashed downstairs to find Mom, just in case she knew anything about A.D.'s flight.

I stayed in his office, and less than a minute later I heard Dad's computer ping with a new email. But this was his work email, and I was told never, ever, ever to look at it, because it was a Federal crime to read his messages, punishable by three years in jail.

So, of course I read the email right away.

It was from that NTSB woman, Becky. She'd sent a series of ID numbers, and the name of a charter company called Kala Air. It must have meant something important, because Becky signed off with a message that said: *"Jake, looks like it's possible your sister's on that plane. I'm fueling an international NTSB jet, and putting an international Go-Team on standby. We're ready to jump on a moment's notice. Best, Becky."*

I printed off the numbers and snuck out of my Dad's study, just as he came running back, asking, "Did my phone ring? Did it?"

I shook my head "no," while looking down, so he wouldn't see that I was up to something.

I was. I had a rendezvous with my iPhone.

I ditched into the bathroom, which is the only room in our house with a lock, which I locked, and I logged into Skype. I saw that Harry and Carly were both online. After taking a deep breath, I group-IM'd them: *Wanna go to Thailand?*

Carly IM'd back: *When, tonight? Cuz I'm supposed to go to Staples with my Mom.*

I sent: *No, Thailand's tomorrow. Tonight we're going to Miami to get back my half of the crystal.*

Carly IM'd back: *Wait, you mean Thailand the country not the take-out food place in town? And Miami the actual city in Florida?? :-Z*

I sent: *Yup. ;-)*

I then sent a long IM and explained that there was a crippled 747 that some truly evil guys had gotten their hands on. I explained that it might be scheduled to take my aunt A.D. home from Thailand and that it would probably crash. I told Harry and Carly how the NTSB was readying a Go-Team, but that if they hadn't figured out the problem by now, they needed my crystal and my Legos.

"Please, you guys," I wrote, "I need you, I really need you, to go on this trip to help me with things I couldn't yet imagine."

It was clear that we needed Harry because he had the credit card, but we also needed Carly because she would be the only one who could calm A.D. down after A.D. found out that three kids had flown halfway around the globe on a fake credit card, using hot-wired iPhones, to save her without telling any of our parents where they were.

I waited for a reply. And waited.

Finally Carly IM'd back: *Wow, that's the longest TXT I ever read. How can U type that fast?*

Then Harry chimed in on Sykpe, and I was actually really, really glad to hear from him. He IM'd: *Count me in! I didn't do my math homework anyway.*

I IM'd back: *Get your passports. Meet me at the barn. Harry, we're gonna need that credit card.*

Harry sent: *Already packed. ;-))))ZZ*

I IM'd to both Carly and Harry: *Don't pack clothes or bring a suitcase or anything when you leave your house. It will only raise suspicion!! We'll use Harry's credit card to buy what we need.*

Harry IM'd: *I'm arranging transportation to the airport. Just meet at the barn.*

Twenty minutes later, Harry, Carly, and I were standing in front of the barn behind my house. I was afraid that if we had to wait too long for the taxi to arrive, someone would chicken out. But then, thanks to Harry, we got another very good reason for starting on our trip: A massive, gleaming-white, 25-foot-long Humvee stretch limo pulled into the driveway. The driver pulled up and rolled down his window, and said, "I'm here to pick up Mr. Obama's party to go to the airport?"

Harry kept a straight face and said, "Yes, that's us. The Obamas, party of three." Then he asked, "And you got my Dad's credit card number over the phone from him?" He emphasized the words *"my Dad's"* so much that the driver was probably on to us.

"Oh sure, we're all set," the driver said, adding with a smirk, "Mr. Obama."

You could tell that he knew we were up to something, but he also seemed to be playing along. Plus, he didn't exactly have a fatherly look about him. Instead of a black business suit like most limo drivers wear, he was wearing reflective aviator sunglasses, a black beret, a lime-green polo shirt with the collar turned up high, and a beat-up leather jacket. From the looks of him, he seemed to be the kind of guy who wouldn't flip out if you threw up in his car – which we weren't planning on doing, but you gotta prepare.

We all popped into the back seat and headed to the airport, but not before I glanced back over my shoulder and simultaneously saw someone at Harry's house *and* Carly's house *and* my house peeking through the curtains as we pulled away.

Oh, that's just freakin' great, I thought. Our parents would be burning up the phone wires in a matter of minutes, and the police would not be far behind. I had to face it – from here on out, we were three outlaws on the run.

Then Carly spoke up, saying what was on all of our minds: "When are we going to tell our parents where we are?"

There was a long silence.

"Simple! "Harry said, "We just tell 'em …that…that"… But he didn't come up with anything.

Then I said, "Yeah, why don't we … Why not … Um, how about we just …"

Then we were all silent, and another, more urgent thought crossed my mind that made me forget about almost everything else.

"Pardon me, sir," I said, leaning forward and tapping the driver on the shoulder. "But could you please stop at the nearest toy store?"

"First of all, it's not sir, it's Sal," he said, offering to shake my hand by turning around in what seemed like a dangerous move, given the fact that he was actually supposed to be driving. He caught my reaction and said, "Aw, come on kid, if we get in a crash, who's gonna get hurt – the guy driving that dinky hybrid with bird wings for doors, or *us* behind the wheel of a 25-foot tank like this baby?" Sal slapped the steering wheel to drive home the point.

"Now, let me get this straight," Sal continued. "You and the other Obamas are on the lam… and you want to go shopping for *toys*? Man, can you give the Transformers and WarHammer 40K a rest for once?"

"Actually, I need Legos," I said.

"You know," Sal said. "That makes me think of the funniest story. I saw on this internet, and it's probably a complete hoax, but you gotta admit this is brilliant. I mean you can't make this stuff up, but there's this kid out there who people say can use Legos to solve…"

But Sal couldn't finish his sentence, as Carly chimed in: "…Who could use his Legos solve airplane crashes."

Then Sal continued. "Oh man, I'd like to lay my eyes on that freak. Probably grew up in a cage in the basement, feasting on Fruit Loops. Head like a mushroom. Wacko goo-goo eyes."

Sal laughed, but now one else did, and his laugh trailed off to an awkward hee-hee-hee.

"Got a rear view mirror, Sal?" Harry asked.

"Read view. Sure," Sal said, a little surprised.

"Take a look in it right now," Harry said. "The guy sitting next to me is the Lego plane crash solving dude."

Sal slammed on the brakes so hard we almost got triple-whiplash. "You're that kid? The Lego kid?" He squinted at me in his rearview mirror.

"But dude, you look perfectly normal. What's with that? I thought you'd look like someone out of *Men In Black 2*, you know with the freaky face, but here you are in my limo looking like someone who's about to ask for a glass of cold milk! Go figure."

Then Sal floored it, throwing all three of us back into our seats, and in seconds we pulled into a Toys R Us. Carly, Harry and I jumped out as Sal yelled, "When you're inside, tell

the manager they have the R backwards on their sign! Bugs me!
And when you come back outside, can you give me your ideas
on the pick 6 lottery numbers for this weekend? No pressure.
You know, best guess, whatever comes to mind."

In under 15 minutes, we'd spent over $900 on Legos for
the trip.

"It's like it's free, with this thing!" Harry said as he
swiped the Visa card, and the charges sailed through. I had
picked up all the Star Wars-themed stuff I could find. But since I
needed other random pieces, I even got stuff that I hadn't even
looked at since I was a little kid. I figured I'd need them all, and
besides, I didn't know how hard it would be to find the right
Lego supplies in Thailand. We jumped back in the limo and
headed to the airport. That's when things started getting *really*
interesting, and Sal was the first to notice.

"Looks like we got trouble," Sal said, as we joined a line
of limos and taxis in the drop-off lane at the airport. There were
two cops at the entrance to the International Departure
terminal, and one was holding a picture of *me,* and looking
through the windows of all the cars coming into the airport.

Our folks must have called the cops. Wow, that was fast.

"Are they after us?" Carly asked. "They must know we're
trying to fly to Thailand. They don't know that we're first
headed to…"

"Don't worry just yet, sister," Sal said, cutting her off. "We have tinted windows. But where are you guys really headed right now?"

"Miami," we all said together. Sal peeled out of the airport, screeching the tires again, and really goosing the gas.

"Plan B!" he said with a sly smile, as he peered into the rearview mirror, watching the cops disappear into the background. Something told me it wasn't Sal's first time making a quick getaway from the police.

"What, we're *driving* to Miami?" Harry asked.

"Nope," said Sal, "the gas bill alone would max that credit card of your 'dad's,'" he said, taking his hands off the steering wheel to make air-quotes with his fingers around the word *dad's*. "But," he continued, "we *are* going to drive to another airport where they won't be looking for you, even if they do think you're not flying to, ah, where was it?"

"Thailand," we all shouted together, growing more excited. "We're going to Thailand!" we screamed again. We howled and whooped as Sal floored it and swerved in and out of traffic. With the pressure off us for the moment, Harry and Carly and I all started discovering some very cool compartments in the limo, one stuffed with jumbo candy bars, another with ice-cold colas, and – Oh, hello, how cool is this? – a remote control that lowered an HD TV screen with premium satellite.

Ah, life on the run!

Chapter Thirteen

Airborne

I woke up with a neck ache, as the sun was just coming up behind our 757-200. Seriously nice plane! Something I could easily get used to. It could easily fit 30 of Sal's Humvee Limos. We were headed due west toward Asia, Thailand, and potentially toward trouble, but definitely and most certainly toward the rescue of my aunt A.D.

For all the trouble we were going to get in for this, our seats sure were nice! Harry had taken the trouble to upgrade us all to first class, and I can tell you, it was worth every stolen dollar we supposedly paid for it. Of course, I say that as someone who was never going to see the Visa card bill. But *whoever* was paying for it, thanks! Pay you back some day.

The last twenty-four hours seemed like a crazy scene from a movie. After we spotted the cops at the airport, Sal drove us about two hours away to another airport, and we waltzed into the place with no cops in sight! Harry whipped out that trusty magic credit card and paid Sal off with a $200 tip, which I guess was a bonus for not actually killing us with his crazy driving. Then, Sal used the Harry's card to get our seats to Miami, and then first class onward to Thailand, pretending to be Harry's dad. You had to admire how he handled it, too…the way he turned to Harry and said, "The window seat, right son? like last time?" Perfect touch. He didn't overdo it either, like by telling the ticket agent, "I'm this young man's farther, in case you're wondering, and I'm treating him and his friends to a trip to Thailand. What an adventure they have in front of them, these youngsters." *That* would have raised some eyebrows, I think.

Before our flight to Miami, we totally junked out on some great food at the airport, all total Mom no-no's: Nathan's hot dogs, Ben and Jerry's…what Harry called "last meal request" food. All that junk food helped soothe the awful feeling we all had in the pits of our stomachs. You know, that feeling you get when you run away from home and you just *know* that your parents are freaking out.

Then, as we had been finishing off our Peace Pops and considering another round of chili fries with extra cheese, Harry said something that made me sad.

"My Mom will be worried about me. *Really* worried," he said. "But my Dad won't be. He doesn't give a rat's ass about me."

Carly and I had looked over in amazement. Harry was straight-faced when he said that, but was he joking? But then, the poor kid actually started to cry. I mean, he really blubbered like a baby. I gave Carly a look that said, *Please make him stop!*

She swung into action, giving Harry a rough, sideways hug and said, "Aw, come on, sport!" and punched him on his arm. She said everything she could think of to get him to shake his bad mood, like "Hey, turn off the waterworks, buddy," and "Wait 'til your Dad sees that credit card bill, and then he'll want you *real* close by!"

She tried her best, but Harry was in full meltdown. Was my Mom right that Harry was just lonely?

I have to admit I actually felt a little sorry for him, but then I spotted an internet café and got a great idea. "Hey, I'm going over there and send an email to my Mom and dad. Just to tell 'em I'm okay. Anyone else...?"

"Great idea!" Carly said. "How about you, Harry? You wanna...?"

But he was already running there. We paid for an hour of computer usage and took turns logging on to our Gmail accounts. We wrote our folks basically the same thing: that we were safe and secure... but on a secret mission we weren't at liberty to discuss, just yet. We also promised them that we'd email them whenever we could finally let them know more. Oh man would that ever make my Mom and Dad stew.

"Unless we're killed or captured by terrorists," Harry had written in the email to his Dad.

"Um, maybe we shouldn't say that," Carly said. "We want to reassure them, not..."

"Good point!" Harry said, showing that he was almost back to normal. He rewrote his email to say *Unless we're killed or captured...*

"I'll leave off the terrorist stuff. For now, Harry said.

"That's thinkin'" Carly said, giving up on the apparently hopeless mission of changing Harry's mind.

When I wrote my parents, I asked them in a "p.s." at the end of the message why they had given the police last year's school picture with my mouth hanging open, when this year's picture was way better. I said I understood that they weren't thinking clearly because they were distraught but, you know, just sayin'... 'cause that kind of stuff ends up in the papers you know. I clicked "Send," and it wasn't more than ten seconds before I got a reply from my Dad. And then almost immediately another popped up from my Mom. They must have had their eyes glued to their own computers waiting to hear from me. But I just deleted both of their messages *unread*. I was afraid they might convince me to come back home immediately. Trust me, they're real pros at that stuff – you know, mind control.

Anyway, I told them that I was okay, and that was the important thing. I'd still catch hell when I got home, sure, but now they wouldn't waste their time on search parties in the woods and stuff.

We had gotten to the Miami airport, and I kind of showed off that I knew where everything was, since I had just been there with my Dad. We took a taxi to the NTSB complex drove right up to the memorial garden, since it wasn't a high-security facility or anything.

I had walked into the garden alone, and sure enough, my crystal was right where I'd left it. Maybe it was because none of us had really slept the night before, but when I leaned over to pick up the crystal, I felt kind of woozy. I brought it back to where Carly and Harry were waiting by the taxi, and they wanted to hold the crystal. So I let them.

Carly just ran her hand over it, as though she were trying to summon a magic genie. She even closed her eyes and whispered something, probably a wish. She even took the necklace that A.D. had given her and touched it to the stone.

Harry, on the other hand, wasn't quite so mystical-minded. He took a picture of it with his iPhone and fiddled with his phone for a sec, which was weird. Who was he sending the picture to? Then he closed his eyes and squeezed the crystal real hard in his hand. He peeked out from one eye, frowned, and then squeezed his eyes shut and squeezed the crystal again. He opened them. He look at me and – almost angry that nothing was happening – he said, "Hate to tell ya, Mr. Mack-gician, that's just a plain old rock and you've been wasting our time. I wished it would dish me up a plate of pancakes, and in case you haven't noticed, nothing happened!"

But then Carly had jumped in: "Harry, maybe it's not the crystal itself but what certain people bring to it. It doesn't work with just anyone, but it obviously works with Mack."

As she handed it back to me, I thought she looked a bit doubtful herself. The truth was, I didn't feel *anything* from the crystal, which surprised me, considering that it had felt almost *alive* at Evers' funeral! I remembered how it seemed to move around from place to place, on its own – from the garden where Mom had thrown it, to under my pillow… for instance. And even before that, from my luggage to the trunk in Evers' attic.

Had I used up its power? Was it like a bank account that had only a certain amount of money in it, and I'd already cleaned it out?

"Hey, Mack, didn't you say you solved the last mechanical failure without the crystal?" Harry asked, still sounding a little p.o.'ed. "How do you account for that? Huh?"

"I can't," I said, "I don't know *how* it works. All I know is that some really strange stuff has happened since my grandfather Evers died, and I've had an even stranger feeling that it was building up to this trip we're about to take."

"You just wanted my Dad's credit card," Harry said bitterly. "That's the only reason you like me now."

"Harry!" Carly said, "that's a *terrible* thing to say! Do you think we'd be risking our lives and yours without something larger out there? Another life to save? Isn't that bigger than all of us? And worth it? With or without the crystal?"

For a second I was afraid Carly would make Harry start crying again, which was all we needed. So I jumped in quick to smooth things over.

"They never believed me either, Harry," I said, "No one here at the NTSB believed me when I told them how those crashes happened. Even my Dad doubted me. My Mom too. But in the next few days my aunt A.D. is scheduled to fly aboard a ticking time-bomb, and we're the only people who can save her. Now, whether you believe the crystal works or not, it comes down to this: Who's with me, and who's getting out of the taxi right now?"

Carly shot her arm up in the air: "With."

Then Harry stuck his arm up in the air, even though it looked like it was killing him. "With," he finally mumbled.

Maybe his doubt was contagious, but at that point I felt the magic of the crystal was lost. I felt *nothing* from it now. It could have been any old rock. What had once been a mystical exchange between me and Evers, where I felt he was returning to earth through me to save people, well, it all seemed so silly now, something that I made up just to make myself feel special… something maybe A.D. and Mom and Dad all played along with just to humor me.

Things didn't get better at the airport. While we were sitting in the departure gate waiting for our flight to Thailand, Harry whispered something to Carly that got her truly agitated. It looked like she was giving Harry a real talking-to, like she was his mother or something. All I actually heard were a few phrases she said to him, like "You can't do that!" and "Are you out of your mind?" and "Take it down, Harry." Now, the first two phrases could be applied to just about any situation involving Harry. But I had no idea what "Take it down!" could mean.

Carly stormed away from Harry and he just looked up mystified. Then Carly turned to me and said, "Don't look now, but Harry's got the crystal on eBay!"

"What?!" I said. "Harry, you're auctioning off my crystal?"

"I'm not auctioning it!" he said, outraged that I'd suggest such a thing. "I set it for 'Buy Me Now' for five million dollars!"

"Is it down now, Harry? Did you take it off?" I asked.

Harry just grumbled to himself. After I asked him a third time, he said, *"I'm doing it."*

*   *   *

My mind snapped back to my present surroundings, and it took me a second or two to remember where that was: aboard the 757-200 that was taking us to Bangkok, the capital city of Thailand. The big jet swopped, making a broad turn, and my stomach fluttered. The rays of sunshine beamed into the cabin, one beam waking Carly, across the aisle from me.

When I turned around to check on Harry, he was really living it up in first class, with a huge breakfast tray. He was also treating the flight attendant as his full-time personal assistant: He said, "Could you heat up that blueberry muffin one more time, love? It's cooled a bit between the first and second bites."

Carly and I looked at each other and just laughed.

Right before we started to drop altitude for our descent into Bangkok, the stewardesses handed out customs forms for us to fill out. The forms had both English and Thai on it, and that was my first glimpse of the Thai script. It looked like organized scribble, and seeing that strange script for the first time made me realize how far we were from home. We hadn't landed, and I was already getting homesick.

"Homesick yet?" Carly asked, as though she were reading my mind. "I am. Kinda. Just a little," she said.

"Me? Homesick?" I said. "Nope, not me."

As the plane made its final descent, Carly, Harry, and I worried that there'd be someone on the lookout for us at the airport. We planned to just play dumb and wait for the first opportunity to duck outside the airport and lose ourselves in the busy streets. It shouldn't be too hard, we thought, because why should anyone here care about three American kids playing hooky from school?

That's what we thought right up to the moment when an announcement came on the plane's loudspeaker, first in Thai, then in English:

"Will all passengers kindly remain in their seats after landing. Airport security personnel wish to check the aircraft…"

There were groans after both the Thai and English announcements, but I wasn't too concerned. "Strictly routine," I assured Carly and Harry. As if I would know.

Then the door to the jet popped open and four armed Thai soldiers *raced* onto the plane. I don't know what Carly and Harry thought, but I'll tell you what I thought: "Cool!" as I looked around to see where the bad guys were.

Turns out the bad guys were *us*, because they came directly to our seats, and one of them firmly asked us to follow them out of the plane. It was hard to take them seriously, because they were so pleasant, and seemed more like actors than real soldiers. Their green fatigues looked brand-new and freshly ironed; even their guns looked a little like toys.

But when Harry took too long responding to their commands, they all got very stern looks on their faces, and one of them pulled out his baton and jabbed him in the ribs. *That* got Harry out of his seat. Then all the soldiers started barking orders at us. These guys meant business!

Chapter Fourteen

Captured, Briefly

We were escorted down a long hallway that was glass on all sides and you could see people by the hundreds waiting there for arriving passengers. Take it from someone who knows: If you ever want to get stared at in an airport, just march three American kids, at gunpoint, down a long corridor. Oh, and have one of them carrying a Battle of Endor Lego set, and another trying to polish off the last of his breakfast muffin.

I told Carly and Harry that maybe this was one of those crazy Asian TV game shows where they trick you into thinking you're going to prison before announcing you'd won ten million yen!

"It's not yen in Thailand," Carly said. "It's *baht*."

"Well, *someone's* been reading her in-flight magazine!" said Harry sarcastically.

We were put in a private holding area. The walls were painted an ugly shade of green, which was exactly the same shade as our school's detention room. Which *proves* that they pick that color deliberately as an extra punishment.

There was a door at the front and one at the back, but we were very clearly locked in, and we felt like prisoners. After maybe half an hour, the door was unlocked and a solider quietly entered the room and placed the rest of our bags in a neat pile on a bench. They'd obviously gone through our stuff. He left, closing the door behind him, and there was some loud talking in Thai in the hallway outside that we couldn't understand.

"He didn't lock the door!" Carly said in a loud whisper.

I moved quietly to the door, and was just about to try the handle, when it was very loudly locked from the outside.

"Good timing, Shakespeare," Harry said.

I was about to point out to Harry that the expression was supposed to be "*Nice play*, Shakespeare," because Shakespeare wrote plays, he didn't make clocks.

But Harry didn't stop there.

"See, the *reason* the door wasn't locked until now," Harry said, "was because the dude who just left the room *lost* his key and had to get someone else to lock the door…"

"Is that right," I said, yawning with boredom. "And you know this *how*, exactly?"

Then Harry started to laugh hysterically, confirming my earlier opinion that he was a nitwit.

"Gee," he said in an exaggerated way, "I wonder where he coulda lost that key?"

He started laughing again, and then made that annoying jingling sound with…

The keys in his hand.

I stared at Harry in wonder as he shook the small key ring he had obviously lifted off the belt of the soldier who had brought in our luggage.

"Bet your magic crystal can't do that, Mr. Mack-gician!"

"Yeah, good work," I said, "but they're standing right outside that door! How can we..."

Carly kind of smirked at me, like I wasn't getting the whole joke or something. Then I finally *did* get it, and felt like a genuine, Class-A nincompoop.

You can't jingle a single key. You need at least two, which meant there were at least two keys on the stolen key ring in Harry's hand. One of them *probably* opened the other door in the back of the room – our escape route!

Before I'd even figured it all out, Carly started grabbing our stuff from the bench, while Harry ran to the back door with the keys.

One of the keys fit the lock. It worked! Without losing even a second, we hurried out. For good luck, I took the crystal out of my pocket and clutched it in my fist.

To our amazement, the back door opened onto a busy Bangkok street, and it was dazzling! As far as we could see to the left and right, there were people jamming the street, many of them Buddhist monks wearing orange-colored robes. There were so many food stalls crammed together that clouds of cooking steam billowed in the air from all over, blinding us now and then.

I stopped to just take it all in. Amazing.

People sat down to eat on upturned buckets anywhere there was room, sometimes right in the street, and there were ducks and chickens and even some little birds roasting on fires made in old metal drums *right there* on the curb.

But there was more for sale here than just food. In just one block, it looked as though you could buy everything you'd ever need: shirts and towels, dresses, sandals and sneakers, flowers, even DVDs. You could buy *anything:* Buddhist statues, incense, lotus blossoms, bright fabric, medicines, bike parts… and it was all jammed together in tiny spaces, with one stall practically tipping over the next one. Behind the stalls that lined the street, more open-air stalls were squeezed between buildings, some as narrow as a doorway. They sold books and toys, or cooking pots, ropes, tools, and glass…

And the noise! All the vendors and customers had to shout to be heard, because of all the buses that roared by, all of which were *way* overloaded with people hanging out of every door. I would have hung out there for an hour if we weren't in danger of being caught.

Carly said we should try our best to blend into the crowd.

"Yeah, right," I said, "that's like telling three elephants to blend into a crowd of miniature circus poodles."

How obvious were we? Picture three American kids, one with long blond hair, all dressed in T-shirts, carrying huge Star Wars Lego sets over their heads. We couldn't have been more obvious if we carried a giant arrow sign pointing to us, with a bullhorn saying, LOOKING FOR THE THREE MISSING AMERICAN KIDS? HERE WE ARE!!

As we walked past the never-ending lines of food stalls and vendors, I just hoped that the soldiers who locked us in the holding room took a *really long* coffee break, or tea break, or whatever they drink here break. Plus, we didn't have the slightest idea where we were going. I had no idea where A.D. was, or even what flight she was taking home. I knew only approximately when she was flying back. But where was she now?

Just when I stopped to turn to Carly and Harry to see what we should do, I noticed a Buddhist monk in saffron robes taking interest in us, as he clutched his long string prayer beads. I guessed he was about my Dad's age, though his shaved head made him appear older. There are tons of monks on the streets of Bangkok, and I wouldn't bother mentioning this one, except for one fact: he had planted himself right in front me on the street and was blocking my path. He just stared at me, smiling slightly as he pointed to my hand. I didn't know what he was getting at, until I looked down and realized he was pointing at my crystal.

Our eyes met, and his smile seemed to say that he knew me. And here's the weird thing: I had a feeling that *I knew him too*. But I *didn't* know him, of course. I couldn't possibly have known him, and so I tried to walk around him. But he gently stepped in my way. I tried again on the other side, but he did it again… and again … and again. Any direction I tried to move, he gently stepped into my path, smiling all the while.

At first, I thought he was crazy, but his calm face eventually convinced me that he meant no harm. Harry and Carly turned around to watch when they saw I wasn't keeping up with them. They both started to get a little nervous, thinking that maybe this monk was an undercover cop. Sounds nuts, sure, but who knew how they did things in Thailand?

Harry spoke up, saying, "Wow, this dude is seriously wacko."

"Harry. He's not wacko," Carly said. "He's a monk. Maybe he just wants to see our Legos."

Then the monk spoke, saying, "The crystal. The crystal," several times while circling his index finger in the air, like he was following the path of a butterfly. "Where did you get my crystal?"

"Did he say *my* crystal?" Harry asked.

Then, all of a sudden, the monk's face changed from a smile of a look of fear.

"Soldiers!" he hissed, pointing behind us. "Are soldiers after you?"

We all nodded *yes*.

"Come this way. Quick!" he said.

For a moment, we didn't know whether we even *should* follow him. Maybe he wasn't a monk at all, but some kind of con-artist. He saw us hesitating, and said in a very insistent voice: "No time to explain. Soldiers coming. This way! This way!"

We looked behind us and he wasn't lying. One of the soldiers who locked us in the holding room was only ten steps behind us. He would soon spot us, so we decided to trust the mysterious monk.

Chapter Fifteen

The Kids in Jail

Butter-fat lamps flickered down a long hallway giving off an eerie light, as Harry, Carly, and I followed the monk.

"This way. This way!" the monk hurried us along.

"A little pushy for a dude in orange pajamas, wouldn't you say?" Harry said.

"Harry, that's what all the monk's wear," Carly said.

"Oh, no. The boy's right. These my PJs," the monk said, surprising all of us.

Harry smirked, *See. Told ya.*

He led us down a very narrow alley between two ancient stone buildings, and then into a tunnel beneath a busy road. Just over our heads we could hear the muffled sounds of cars and trucks and the softer *tuk-tuk-tuk* sound of the three-wheeled taxis that are actually called *tuk-tuks* in Thailand.

We all ducked through a small doorway that looked like it was made for dwarves instead of people, and we came into a room where we saw something so enormous and unreal that I nearly couldn't believe my eyes. It was a huge statue of the Buddha, maybe 150 feet long. But he was sleeping on his side, his head resting on one huge arm. As if he were having a nice dream, the statue was grinning. It looked very familiar. Like

Evers' grin. Like our statue at home. Very interesting. All three of us stood there staring, forgetting for a minute that we were fugitives.

"Oh yes, Sleeping Buddha," the monk said all casual like in passing, like my mother would say, 'Oh yeah, the Swifter. I saw the infomercial; thought I'd try it." Nothing special. Just another 150 foot statue of a sleeping mystic.

He escorted us behind a heavy curtain and into a back room, where other monks sat reading from small books and chanting prayers. We sat and rested for the first time in what seemed like hours, laying our bags and Lego boxes aside, and accepted short glasses of cool water from some curious young monks that walked over.

"Look! Star Wars Legos," one of the Monks said in English, "Cool."

Our jaws dropped when we realized that they knew English, but we were more astounded that they knew what Star Wars Legos were. "I loved all those movies, especially Anakin's car race in *The Phantom Menace*," he said.

We just stared and smiled.

Finally the older monk sat down next to us, nervously looking out the windows and drawing the curtains to keep out the bright, tropical midday sunlight.

He held out his hand for me to shake and said, "I'm Krit."

Krit... Kirt... Why did that name sound so familiar? I immediately flashed back to my conversation with Evers, just before he died. Evers had said: *"A young Monk named Krit gave this to me, Mack, and I want you to have it,"* referring to his crystal.

I remembered Evers telling me that the young monk was just a kid when Evers met him in Thailand. Now he was obviously very grown-up.

"I think I know you me," Krit said to me. "I mean, I think I know someone in your family. Your grandfather, perhaps?" I nodded and he smiled, then looked at the crystal I held in my hand.

Krit said, "It was bigger then, the crystal. Looks as though you have just half of it."

I was about to explain to him that my aunt A.D. had the other half.

But Krit spoke before I could say anything: "And now the crystal has brought you to me, again serving as a means of escape, of keeping order," he said. "Funny. It has come full-circle."

He made a circular motion with his two arms, swinging them broadly around, his hands meeting just in front of his face.

I was still a little suspicious of him. I mean, was he who he said he was? And those other monks? Were they really monks at all? Just the fact that they were Star Wars fans made it seem a bit unreal. I was trying to figure out a way to test if this was the real Krit. But just when I remembered to quiz him about Roland, to see if he knew him too, I heard an odd scuffling noise. I looked up to see that the three young monks who were sitting nearby were looking in my direction, but they were focused very determinedly on the crystal in my hand.

I turned to Krit and smiled nervously, but when I turned back, the three young monks had moved closer and were bowing to me with their hands together, as if they were praying.

"Dude," Harry said, "they think you're Yoda!"

Carly looked on wearily and said "Something odd this way comes," in a froggy Yoda voice.

I was just about to ask Krit if he knew anything about A.D. After all, she may have visited the same temple where he grew up, and she had the other half of the crystal. But before I could say anything, a beam of light speared into the temple, shining directly into our eyes, like someone was purposely trying to blind me.

Before I knew it, a dozen Thai soldiers swarmed around us, and we were face down. It all happened so fast we couldn't even yell out for help, much less run away. We were handcuffed. Handcuffed! And in a Buddhist temple! Were they even allowed in here?

Krit and the monks looked on helpless, but they really couldn't intervene, and everyone knew it. The soldiers even bowed respectfully to the monks, making a sign of prayer with their hands, just before marching us away.

I thought back to when we first saw the people streaming through the streets of Bangkok, and how they seemed to sway like sea-grass, waving back and forth in unison with whatever tide moved them. The monks seemed to bend that way now too, yielding to the "tide" of the uniformed men rushing through the room, and waiting calmly to spring back up when that force had passed. It was then that I did something really risky. I didn't want the crystal to fall into the wrong hands. So I let it go when I was bending down to pick up my bags, rolling it away from me. Krit saw this, and moved his leg so that his robes hid the crystal. He winked at me and made a prayer sign with his hands as the soldiers led us away.

The soldiers pushed us through the thick traffic in the Bangkok streets, but it turned out we weren't going back to the airport holding area. In fact, we weren't going back to the airport at all. One soldier was clearly in charge and he got a call on his cell phone; but he mostly listened and then hung up. He shouted orders to the other soldiers, and they hustled us off double-time to a nearby police jail.

I was getting used to being held by armed men. Machine guns aimed at me? That was "just another day at the office." But I was a bit scared when they separated us. Carly, Harry, and I were all split up, and they took our bags, even the Legos. I mean, really, we were in Thailand to save lives, not hurt anyone! Weren't they taking this a little too seriously? All we were really guilty of was using Harry's fake credit card. Oh, yeah, and stealing the policeman's key to the holding room. Oh, and escaping police custody, and evading the police. And hiding in the sacred temple. All right, maybe there *was* a little more for them to be upset about.

They took us down a long, quiet corridor – *way* too quiet for supposedly being in the center of one of the busiest cities in the world – and they put us in three separate cells. But this time, the cells didn't have regular doors. They had iron bars instead, which were covered with rusty metal fencing. The bars were locked from the outside. So swiping the guard's keys wasn't an option.

The cell they locked me in was tiny and hopeless looking. There was only one window, up high, and the bed was an old mattress that had bugs scurrying across the top and sides. Yuck. That became a double yuck when the day grew long and boring, and as the light faced, I realized that I'd be spending the night right where I was sitting. Who knows what Carly and Harry went through? Probably the same thing, and the only peep I heard out of *anyone* was Harry's voice of outrage when – just after a guard dropped off a simple dinner of rice and chicken – Harry yelled into the hallway: "Any chance at all for seconds on the chicken?"

The next morning one of the Thai soldiers stopped outside the bars of my cell and said something in Thai to someone I couldn't see at first. Then he unbolted and opened the barred door and a tall, kind of scrawny American man in a tan colored business suit came into my cell. He smiled with thin, tight lips as the soldier closed and bolted the barred door again behind him.

"Mack," the American man said, finally smiling a bit and reaching out to shake my hand. "I'm John Hannigan, from the U.S. Embassy."

I just looked at him blankly for a second. I wasn't even fully awake, and I didn't even know what to say. I was glad he was an American and could maybe help us get out. But I just blinked there in the hot silence, waiting for him to tell me what kind of trouble we were in.

It turned out he had a fairly complete knowledge of everything we'd done to break the law.

"Son," he said, "you're in a troublesome spot. The whole credit card thing could probably have been forgotten. But the stealing of the keys. The escape. That's stuff you just can't do. Not in the U.S., and not here either. People get real touchy when you break the law like that. It's a sign of disrespect."

I just stared at him, but now it was hard for me to keep my mouth shut. Suddenly I was *dying* to tell him why we were there, why we escaped, and what we had to do... what I was *determined* to do, with or without the permission of the Thai soldiers or the U.S. Embassy, or even of my mom and dad. And that was to find A.D. and get my crystal back, and then find that bad 747 – even if I had to get on it myself – and use my Legos to keep it from crashing.

"First things first, okay?" he said, as he took a cell phone out of his pocket. He asked for my home number and dialed. I held the phone to my ear, and my Mom answered before the phone finished ringing even once. She spoke in a burst of words. I was really surprised, because instead of being happy to hear from me, she was, like, soooo mad.

She started out okay, crying and saying stuff like, "Mack. Mack. Oh Mack, you're all right!" Then she suddenly switched gears: "How could you *do* this to your Dad and me? We had no idea if you were dead of alive. Have you lost your... Where are you now?"

"Um, I think I'm in jail," I said. "In Bangkok."

"*In jail?!*" she said, "what did you... How on earth did you end up there? We had police in three states on high alert for you. Are they taking good care of you? Are they sending you home?"

"I don't know," I said. "There's a guy from the embassy here, and he's very nice, and he's going to do what he can, I guess. Mom, I'm staying here..." I started to say.

"Oh, no you're not staying there! You're on the next flight home my friend…" she said.

"Let me finish, Mom. I'm *not* leaving Thailand until I know that plane is safe, that crippled 747. Where's Dad? Is he there?"

"He's on the way to Thailand now. To get you. And to heck with that stupid plane. That's for professionals, Mack. For the police. You've forgotten that you're just a boy, Mack, and this is serious business you're meddling in. Dad says there are criminals involved with that plane, and they're hiding the fact that the plane is broken. Plus, you've broken international law, Mack. The Thai government is probably debating putting you in jail. It's serious business, and that's to say nothing of how sick I've been with worry, Mack. Sick."

"I'M NOT A LITTLE BOY, MOM!" I yelled. I said it so loud that even John Hannigan looked up in surprise.

Mom was silent.

But with that, the Thai solider came back in, speaking Thai to John Hannigan. Luckily, he signaled to me that he had to have his phone back. Best thing that happened to me all day, because it was a foolproof excuse to get off the phone with my Mom. "Oops. Sorry Mom, gotta go," I said, "they're taking the phone back now. Bye. Bye Mom. Can't hear you. Gotta go."

John Hannigan took the phone and I could hear him talking to my Mom. I could easily guess what she was saying, even though I couldn't hear her.

"Oh sure, Mrs. McCarthy," Hannigan said. "I'm going to do all I can to get him out of here and back to the embassy."

Then he tried to lighten the mood by making a little joke. "And we'll try to get the jail sentence reduced to under two years. Mrs. McCarthy... Mrs. McCar... Mrs... It was a joke, ma'am. Yes, yes, you're right, it's no laughing matter. Just trying to interject a little humor in the... Yes, I'll keep an eye on him the entire time. And Carly. Yes, and Harry. Your husband and I will speak when he lands, and we'll try to get all this resolved."

It was just when John Hannigan had started to crack his joke about the jail time that something caught my eye. Someone was peeking into my cell from the tiny window up above us. Mr. Hannigan had his back to the wall, so he couldn't have seen it, and I only caught the tiniest glimpse before it was gone. Weird, but I thought I recognized the person's face. But no, it couldn't be. No way. Not him. Not in a million years!

Chapter Sixteen

A Gathering Force

Jake McCarthy's NTSB jet, a Gulfstream G5, banked sharply to head southwest after departing the Narita airport in Japan. Jake and his team of two pilots had refueled there before the last leg of their flight to Bangkok. Jake had been sleeping on and off during the long leg of the flight from the U.S., but now he awoke and was pouring over a series of computer printouts he had stuffed in his briefcase just before he left.

"There has to be a connection here, and I'm going to find it," he said quietly to himself.

Even in the age of advanced computers and the Internet, Jake often worked with paper and pencil to try and solve particularly difficult problems, like this one. He drew lines from one set of serial numbers to the next. He examined an old spare parts report for the broken 747, trying to trace where the parts had been shipped. If he could determine the 747's new serial number, he could track the plane. But the criminals who had put the crippled plane back in the air probably retagged their plane with a new serial number, or no serial number at all.

Then Jake discovered something odd. Here was a serial number for a retired plane that had never taken out of service.

"That's odd," he said to no one.

He circled the number 171-25R-056-02.

Then he drew more lines between that number and anything the looked like a match, even a partial match.

Still, he couldn't come up with anything conclusive.

The cockpit door opened and out stepped Jake's old friend, Gene Coyle, the co-pilot on the flight to Bangkok, and a lieutenant colonel in the Air Force. Looking as though he was badly in need of a haircut, Gene had a long Irish face, flushed red cheeks, and a mischievous toothy smile that never seemed to go away. He had been a helicopter pilot in the Gulf War, but switched to jets after that because, as he said, "helicopters didn't go fast enough."

Of course, Gene was up on all the latest aircraft technology, but he prided himself on being a skilled pilot who could handle any plane in just about any situation. He'd flown Jake to many crash site investigations, and they had developed the kind of close friendship that could only be forged by two people who had witnessed disaster and death together.

Gene plopped down next to Jake's seat and stared at the sheets of paper, before looking up at Jake. That's when he saw real distress in Jake's face, a sense of distress that had nothing to do with the old spare parts reports on Jake's lap.

"I've known you a long time," Gene said, "and I have to say, you have a look on your face that I don't recognize, a look I've never seen before. It's a look of fear."

"I'm worried about Mack, Gene," Jake said, burying his head briefly in his hands with exhaustion. "It's not like him to pull a crazy stunt like this. I've been trying to distract myself with some work, but I can't stop worrying about where he is, or if he's run into trouble. We just got that one email from him and…"

Gene put his hand on Jake's shoulder and squeezed it as though he were Jake's father.

"Jake, I'm not just saying this to make you feel better," Gene said, "but I have a strong hunch that Mack's going to be okay. He's got a good head on his shoulders, which he obviously got from his mother and not from you."

Just then, Rick Swanson, the co-pilot broke in over the loudspeaker. "Jake," he said, "we've got a satellite call coming in. It's good news. I'll put it through."

Jake perked up when he heard the voice of his wife: *"Jake, can you hear me, it's Lily!"*

"Lily, hi, sweetie, yeah, I can hear you loud and clear. Any news? Anything at all about Mack?"

Gene looked up anxiously now, too. Jake was obviously eager to hear something positive.

"Mack called from Thailand," Lily said. "He called from the cell phone of a fellow at the U.S. Embassy."

"Thank goodness. Is he okay? Is he all right?" Jake asked.

"Well, physically he's all right. But he's in custody of the military."

"The what?" Jake yelled in amazement.

"Yes, he's being held by the Thai government. I talked to this fellow from embassy, John Hannigan, and he's trying to work it out. But apparently Mack, Carly, and Harry not only got into Thailand with a stolen credit card, but they escaped the police after breaking out of an immigration holding area."

"What was he thinking? Jake said, "This is Thailand we're talking about, and they live by different rules there."

Gene looked on shaking his head and said, "Mack sounds a little like his old man, if you ask me!"

"What?" Lil said, "Who's that? Gene?"

"Yeah, Lil, hi," Gene said over the speaker phone. "Listen, I know you two are totally worked up over this thing, but we're going to be in Thailand in less than an hour. Sounds like Mack's safe, he's okay, and we just have to work out the legal logistics to get him home. I seriously doubt they'll put three good kids in jail. The Thais are famous for scaring the heck of kids like this, but jail is not in the picture. As long as they don't keep getting deeper into trouble, that is."

"Oh, Gene, thanks, I'm glad to know you're there," Lil said, sounded relieved.

"Hey, Lil," Jake said, cutting back into the conversation, "I have a satellite connection for my laptop, so can you email me the details you heard from Mack? Send me everything you know that's going on in Thailand, along with the name and cell number of that guy at the embassy. As soon as I land, I'll call him, okay? Now, any word from A.D.?"

"No, not a word," Lil said. "I did call Carly's parents – they're sick with worry, as you can imagine—and I got Harry's mom, who was so upset she called Harry's dad, who she hasn't been in touch with for ages. I mean, just think how we'd react if Carly's parents called us out the blue and said, 'Oh, by the way, Mack went with Carly and this guy Harry to Southeast Asia using a fake credit card and they're on the run from Thai military.'"

Jake laughed at the absurdity of it all.

"Thanks for dealing with that, Lil," Jake said. "I can't imagine it was easy."

Then Lil grew kind of quiet and pensive and said, "This is scaring me, Jake, and I don't just mean Mack running off to Thailand and getting arrested. It's everything else: the crystal, the Legos, Mack's power…"

Jake was silent for a moment. It was the first time he'd heard Lil refer to Mack's power, as if she was finally beginning to accept the possibility he actually *had* powers.

"It scares me a little too, honey," he said, "but I also think it saved our lives on our flight back from Miami. Maybe Mack has other lives to save before this is finished."

And with that they said their goodbyes. Jake looked a little more upbeat and smiled at Gene.

"Tell me something, old friend," Gene said.

"Yeah?" Jake said.

"You really think Mack's got these… these powers?"

Jake thought a minute before answering. "To be honest with you," Jake aid, "every time I convince myself that it's all a fluke, Mack does something that completely changes my mind and makes me believe. Now, that time in Miami, when he couldn't solve the crash at the site, I really put the pressure on him, because it was so important to me, and I was worried that if he didn't pull it off, *I'd* look like an idiot."

"Sure," Gene said. "Which you did, by the way…"

"Well, now I'm thinking *that* was the fluke, *that* was the one time it didn't work, because in every other situation when he's had the chance to solve a crash – even when he didn't know he was solving a crash, like in my Colorado crash research – it seemed that – man, I don't know how else to put it – it seems as though someone or something is speaking through Mack."

"And all this started when your Dad died?" Gene asked.

Jake nodded *yes*. "I have this really strange feeling that my Dad's directing us in some way. I told you that the crystal originated in Thailand, and A.D. has half of it. Right now, she's trying to return it where my Dad got it."

"A.D. is finally burying Evers' spirit, in a way. Is it that kind of thing?" Gene asked.

Jake nodded, a bit bewildered. "Gene, don't you think it's weird that less than two weeks after my Dad died, all these things have happened. Mack has solved three air crashes, and all these people related to Evers – Mack, A.D., me, and even these other kids – we all seem to be gathered in some way by some weird force in Thailand."

But before Gene could answer, the loudspeaker system came back on and the copilot asked Gene to come up to the cockpit to prepare the jet to enter Thai airspace.

Chapter Seventeen

Escaping. Again.

The holding cell door was already loose on its hinges.

That's the first thing Harry discovered soon after he was locked inside his cell and the soldiers left the corridor. The bolts were sunk in cement, but the cement was old and cracked and the bolts were rusted. All the door really needed was a little encouragement to come loose. So Harry looked around the small cell to see what he could use, because it was time for a little jail break.

"It's no different than when I escape from being grounded at Dad's," Harry thought to himself. "I have these soldier dudes like *soooo* fooled. This'll be a cinch."

But Harry couldn't break out barehanded. He needed a tool, even a crude one. And there was nothing in his tiny cell except a bed, and it wasn't like he could just pick up the bed and use it like a battering ram to knock the door off its hinges. He wasn't *that* strong, even for an eleven-year-old. Well, eleven and a half.

But…

Maybe he could use the metal bedpost. So, he kicked at it, Tae Kwon Do style – all that training *finally* came in useful – and he soon detached it from the frame. Still, Harry had to hurry, because that Mr. Hannigan guy said he'd be coming back shortly, right after he talked with Mack and Carly.

Harry worked as quiet as he could, angling one end of the bedpost and to chip away at the cement around the hinges. Whole chunks fell away and within minutes, he was able to pull away the hinged side of the door, opening a narrow passage that he could just squeeze through.

It was *too* easy, Harry thought. It was like someone *wanted* him to escape, the way the wall fell away so quickly to his improvised tool. Quiet as a ghost, he stepped out into the empty hallway, but as he came up to the cell where Mack was captive, he heard Mack talking on the phone. It sounded like… Yep, it sure was… Mack was clearly talking to his mom, and then he heard John Hannigan telling Mack to give him the phone back. He clearly heard John Hannigan speaking to Mack's Mom. Harry tried to keep out of sight, slinking along the wall, working his way to Carly's cell. But first he grabbed a chair and stood up to the window that looked down on Mack's cell, and glanced in there, trying not to be seen. It was then that he heard John Hannigan say something that made his blood run cold.

That was it. They had to get out of here, and fast!

He tip-toed back up to Carly's cell, where she sat alone on the bed.

"Carly!" he whispered fiercely. *"Carly!"*

She looked up immediately.

"They let you out!" she said excitedly, smiling in amazement.

"Shhhh! Not exactly," he said as he slowly and quietly pulled back the security bolt on her cell door.

"What do you mean, 'not exactly'? You mean you…" Carly's face dropped as she understood how Harry had managed to appear at her door.

"Oh no, Harry, *no way*," Carly said. "I am not going to escape again. No way. We'll only get in more trouble."

"They're talking about giving us jail time! Here in Thailand!" Harry said.

"What?"

"Yeah, I just heard that Hannigan guy from the embassy telling Mack's Mom on the phone that he'd try to keep our jail term to under two years!"

Carly suddenly looked frightened.

"Mr. Hannigan said that? " Carly said, "But he told me he'd work it all out, that we could all go home soon."

"And you believed him?" Harry said dismissively. "He probably just said it to keep us quiet, so we don't try to bust out again. He's conning us! We don't know what he's saying in Thai to the police, but I guarantee you it's not the same as he's telling us in English."

"Two years in jail?" Carly said, finally sounding truly scared. "I can't…"

"Sshh!" Harry signaled her to wait while he had his ear cocked. "Somebody's coming," Harry said. "C'mon, Carly, it's now or never!"

Carly hesitated a moment, and she might have hesitated longer if Harry hadn't grabbed her hand and yanked her out of her cell. They both turned and ran like the wind toward the door at the end of the hallway. Then they burst through the door and out the building, just as they heard the soldiers sounding the alarm with loud yelling. They didn't need to understand the Thai language to know what was being said this time.

John Hannigan burst into the hall to see what the fuss was all about, with Mack right behind him – only to see a team of soldiers running past, this time with guns at the ready.

"Let's get Carly and Harry, so we can wrap this up," John Hannigan said to Mack, a little baffled by all the commotion. Then one of the Thai soldiers stopped to say something that Mack didn't understand, but John Hannigan understood it. He held his head in his hands briefly in disbelief, then turned to Mack and said, "I don't believe it! They've escaped again!"

"What? Who? Carly and Harry?" asked Mack, knowing the answer before he finished asking the question.

John Hannigan nodded and rubbed his forehead, as if it ached with stress. "They blew it. I'm not sure I can do much for them now, Mack. This is going to make the Thai authorities really pissed."

Mack couldn't believe it. Why would Harry and Carly run now? Then it came to him in a flash – the face he saw at the window when Hannigan was on the phone with his Mom. He had thought it looked like Harry, but dismissed the thought immediately because it seemed impossible. Harry was supposed to be in a locked cell. Had Harry overheard Hannigan's joke about jail time and taken it seriously?

Hannigan's phone rang. He answered and spoke quickly in Thai, and then hung up and spoke to Mack.

"Okay, we got one piece of this worked out. That was the embassy travel rep. We're sending you home on a plane tonight, Mack. *Tonight*, my friend, without any more delay."

"Why don't we just fly back on my Dad's plane?" Mack asked.

"Well, I'm afraid he's come all this way for no reason, because I think I have this cleared up," Hannigan said. "Cleared up, that is, if I can get you kids to stop escaping. You're all going to fly on a regular charter jet, this time in the economy seats," John Hannigan added, winking to let Mack know that he knew everyone had flown over in first class.

"But what about my aunt? I need to find her!" Mack said.

Hannigan gave Mack a frustrated look.

"I know you're concerned about her," he said, "and you're being a devoted nephew and all. But we have no idea where your aunt is, none. Last we heard, she was trekking up around Chiang Rai, headed off into the jungles on an elephant. Our embassy sources have an eye out for her, but honestly Mack, I'm just not sure I understand how this all ties together. You're getting these ideas that she is in danger from some kind of rock?"

"It's a rose crystal. A *magical* rose crystal actually. Not a rock. And there *is* a real danger of a jet crashing if we don't find it in time, and we're worried it's the plane my aunt is supposed to be on tonight…"

John Hannigan turned the palms of his hands up to the sky in exasperation. He was just about to speak when he heard more yelling down the hall. He understood what was being yelled by the soldiers, and moaned saying, "Oh no…"

"What?" Mack asked. "What happened?"

"Evidently, your two friends aren't in the building. They got away, and the soldiers came back for their rifles," Hannigan said, and suddenly he lost his temper. "Do you guys think this is a neighborhood game of hide-and-seek? These Thai soldiers are armed. You've tricked them. And they *don't* all speak English. If Harry or Carly get cornered, and they turn and say, 'don't shoot,' the soldiers might take that as a sign of aggression."

Mack stared at John Hannigan, amazed that he seemed more concerned about the feelings of Thai police than the safety of Carly and Harry. He was saved from having to come up with something to say, because the door opened down the hall, and Mack's Dad came rushing in.

Mack expected his Dad to just start yelling, but nope, he didn't even say hello. He just hugged Mack long and hard. Mack even worried that maybe his Dad would start crying again, like he did when Evers died. He finally spoke, as he held Mack tightly by the shoulders at arm's length to look him over. "Are you okay? Did anyone hurt you?" he asked.

Mack just shook his head *no*.

"Well, thank God you're all right," he said in relief. "Thank God you're all right," he said again, finally letting go. He turned to John Hannigan, who was looking on a bit impatiently. Jake had obviously gotten to know him through the phone calls they'd had over the last few days.

Jake shook his hand, and said, "A pleasure to finally meet you in person this time. Thanks for all the satellite phone calls to make these arrangements, John. Jeez, kids on the run, and magic crystals, I can't believe this is a typical day for you."

"Well," Hannigan said a bit stiffly, "I have to say that this situation is one of the more, how shall we say, *unusual* ones I've run into. But we'll have you and Mack on a plane tonight, so you can get home safe and—"

"Where are Carly and Harry?" Jake asked.

"Well, Mr. McCarthy," John Hannigan said, now stiffer than ever, "I had *arranged* to put them on the same plane with you, but, well, just before you got here, before I had the chance to explain to them that I had their release all worked out…"

"They escaped," Mack finished for him.

"Yes, they escaped," Hannigan said, giving Mack a quick glare that said, *I can finish my own sentences, thank you very much.*

"Escaped?" Jake said. "From here? How could they? This place is swarming with soldiers. Can we help find them?"

"I'm afraid not," Hannigan said, "It's entirely in the hands of the Thai military."

Hannigan took a deep breath and continued, "I only hope the soldiers don't overreact when they find them. Last time we had a situation like this, one of the kids ended up going home in an air ambulance."

Chapter Eighteen

Legos Everywhere

"Legos!" A.D. exclaimed as she made her way down the aisle of the bus from Chang Rei to Bangkok. She had spotted a twelve-year-old Thai boy who had just opened a massive Space Police Lego set. "My nephew Mack just loves Legos!" A.D. said to him, as if he spoke English.

Then she suddenly realized she was in rural Thailand, where it was very odd to see *any* kind of Western toys, let alone the latest Lego set.

She stopped for a second in the aisle and stared; the boy just looked up and smiled.

"You don't see those Lego sets around much up here. Where'd you get those?" A.D. asked. "Where'd you find them?"

But the boy didn't speak any English. He laughed at her funny way of talking and just went back to playing. It seemed to A.D. that he was starting to make a section of a large airplane.

She found a seat in the back of the bus and started to spread out her things for the long overnight bus ride to Bangkok. She set down her water bottles, a candy bar for later, and some rice. She had found a very curious book at the bus station called *A Short History of Spontaneous Assemblies.*

"Well that's an odd book to find out here in the jungle," she'd said, when she bought it.

But she was more anxious to get her diary updated with the remarkable things that had happened to her over the last three days.

With the honk of its horn, the old bus lurched forward on the dusty road that would lead south. A.D. looked out the window for a minute and then started to write in her diary as the bus bumped along:

Dear Diary:

Let me take you back a few days, because I have tons to tell you. I had taken a trip up to the northern part of Thailand in hopes that I'd find the same monastery where my father, Evers, had visited many years ago. This is the monastery that Evers was staying at when my Mom first got so sick. She died pretty much at the moment when my Dad returned from his trip here. It's a sad memory. Her death was a disruption in the order of things, I think. You see, her own Mom and Dad were still alive then, and, well, kids aren't supposed to die before their parents, no matter how old the kids are and no matter how old the parents are. It's not right, no matter where in the world you go.

Now, with my own Mom and Dad gone, an order will be preserved when I move on to the next world. I am not saying that I want to die any time soon. Oh, no! But I'm next in the order and I don't mind that.

Anyway, this monastery I was trying to visit was the same one where Evers was given a powerful rose crystal, the crystal that broke in half when my Mom died. One piece is with Mack now, a gift from Evers just before he died, and the other piece was with me. I'm not even sure what the true limits of the crystal are yet, but with only half of the original stone, Mack seems to have used it to determine why certain airplanes crash. I have to admit the crystals' powers are not new to me. When I was a kid, I was able to tap into its power, but only partially. Only now do I see that the power the rose crystal gives is different to each person who has it. For Mack, it's airplanes. For me, it was a power that I didn't understand until I got back to the monastery where the crystal came from originally. To get there, I trekked and trekked. After days wandering through jungles where the leaves of the trees were as big as elephant ears, and through grasslands where the edges of the grass were sharper than most knives… and after getting confusing directions as to where exactly the monastery was, I finally walked down a trail and found it, on the banks of the river that Evers and Roland had spoken of.

The trees and plants had overgrown the monastery in the intervening thirty years since my dad's visit here. But it was just as my Dad had described it, with caves carved into the limestone cliffs. The caves were where the monks lived. Turns out that the monk named Krit no longer lives there. He'd moved on to Bangkok, to live at Wat Po, a large city temple that houses the massive and famous Sleeping Buddha statue. But one monk I met even remembered Roland and my Dad, if you can even believe it! He said that as a young boy he had watched Roland gather material for a raft, and that all the monks were laughing like crazy because Roland didn't know that just below the monastery, along the river, just out of earshot, was a massive waterfall that would have swamped them, and broken up the raft… along with a few bones as well. The monk said that they would never have let Evers and Roland go on the raft, but they wanted to watch them build it, just for fun. That same monk was a little older than me, and I sat with him for a long time one day. After getting to know him, and teaching him some English words that he wanted to learn, I sensed I could trust him, and so I pulled the crystal out of my belly pack. His eyed widened and he said something very odd. At first, it seemed like a string of meaningless words: Gahn jaht rah!

I didn't really understand what that meant, until he translated his own words to halting English: "The order! The order of things!"

Are Mack's power to solve crashes preserving the order of things from being disturbed by death? Maybe my sense of calm came from knowing that after my Mom died, the order would be preserved.

At that point, I was a little spooked, which is kind of hard to do to me, but I handed my half of the crystal back to the monk, who looked surprised. His face seemed to question me, but for some reason I really wanted the crystal returned. Then I left my backpack with the monk and took a long walk into the jungle with a feeling that a circle had been closed in my life.

A.D. stopped writing and looked out the window of the bus, lost in thought. With the steady drone of the bus' engine, along with the fast-approaching darkness, she grew sleepy and started dozing off, but not before she tucked her diary into her backpack. She once again looked up the aisle of the bus to see if that little boy still working on his Legos.

And he was! Even this late at night.

In fact, the small reading light above his seat was the only one turned on in the bus, because everyone else had gone to sleep. The light was bright but focused only on the boy, and that made her think that it looked like a beam right from heaven. Before A.D. knew it, she fell into a dreamless sleep.

Hours later, the bus jolted her awake as it lurched into increasingly heavier traffic. A.D. thought she'd been asleep for a short time, but she was surprised to see that it was already dawn.

"I must have slept through the night," she said to no one.

As the bus got nearer to Bangkok, it joined other trucks and cars and buses, all making their ways to the big city. A.D. was astonished at the traffic – *Where are they all coming from?* she wondered – as lines of buses and trucks, all spewing diesel smoke, lined up as though in a parade. At first, they seemed to be racing each other along the two-lane highway, jockeying in and out of lanes of traffic, sometimes even dangerously passing each other by veering on and off the shoulder of the road. But then the traffic grew thicker, and finally, with all the building congestion just miles from Bangkok, everything slowed to a crawl. The only thing that was getting through were the motorcycles, some with three people on them, that weaved in and out of traffic, darting and streaking like frightened fish through the very tight spaces between cars, trucks, and buses.

Looking out the window, A.D. could very clearly see the people in the buses next to her. They were actually just a few feet away.

But then something caught her eye.

Wow, she thought, *that's odd*, as she looked at the bus next to hers. There was another boy, on the bus next to hers, sitting in a window seat building Legos! The longer she looked, the more it seemed as though the boy was working on a section of a Lego airplane. The boy even looked over at A.D. and smiled, as his bus pulled slightly ahead of hers.

Then A.D. got up and walked to the front of her bus to see if that other little boy with the Legos had gotten off this bus, but there he was, sleeping, with a partially constructed Lego airplane section on his lap.

Shaking her head in bewilderment, A.D. went back to her seat and sat there with a very calm and satisfied grin, trusting of the future, but unable to figure out what all this meant.

"Legos seemed to have taken over the entire known world for some reason!" she said out loud to no one.

Chapter Nineteen

On The Run

Carly and Harry didn't last long on their run from the Thai soldiers. Harry somehow imagined their daring escape would be just like Indiana Jones, and they'd leap into the back of a truck that would take them to a secret cave guarded by friendly natives.

Yeah right.

It started out okay. In fact, it was kind of fun, bursting out of jail.

"Nice!" Harry had high-fived Carly when finally realized they were free. "Did you see the looks on the faces of those dudes? We totally baffled them. Jezz…"

But then Carly asked the obvious: "Harry, where are we going?"

"Always hung up in the details. Honestly Carly." Harry said.

But Harry had a sinking feeling in his belly. He just didn't want to admit it. What had earlier been the friendly, teeming streets of Bangkok, with its exotic sights, now seemed a strange and unfriendly place. The river of people that so fascinated them earlier now seemed like unruly mob that shoved them along against their will — at one point forcing Carly into the street where an overcrowded bus nearly mowed her down.

"Watch out!" Harry screamed, yanking Carly back onto the sidewalk.

Harry turned away and walked off before Carly could get his attention to show him that she was just about to cry.

Truth was, neither Harry of Carly knew where they were, or where they were going, and of course they didn't speak the language.

"Harry, maybe we should just go back and turn ourselves in?" Carly said.

"No way!" Harry said, at last spinning around to face her. But what he was really bugging him wasn't the fear of prison or the soldiers, but the fear of returning home to face the wrath of his Mom and especially his Dad.

He couldn't admit that to Carly, of course. Not only would it make him look like a baby, but it would be like admitting that his brilliant escape plan had been a genuinely stupid idea.

He grabbed Carly's arm and actually dragged her forward, even as he knew in his heart that the Thai soldiers would eventually win this one, and they would all have to fly home sometime soon. He cringed when he thought about it, because he'd have to admit to his parents that he'd stolen the cell phones and used a fake credit card for an international, first-class wild goose chase.

"Do... do you know where we're going?" Carly insisted.

"Quit asking me that!"

"But *do* you?" Carly said.

"Of course I do!" Harry said.

Of course he didn't. But he couldn't admit that now.

Then, after blocks of struggling through the waves of people on the sidewalks, they got their first break.

Harry looked up and almost couldn't believe it himself. He held back from screaming out, *"I can't believe it—look!"*

Instead he just turned to Carly, smiling in a self-satisfied way, and "casually" directed Carly with the wave of his hand in the direction of the only city landmark they knew, almost as though he were ushering Carly to her front-row seat in the theater, *this way young lady...*

"Omigosh," Carly said. "Harry, that's Wat Po!"

"Of course it is," Harry said, pretending to have known all along where they were headed. "Where else do you think I was headed?"

She gave him a little smirk, and he felt an enormous sense of relief that she didn't make him admit they had been hopelessly lost.

They walked on, making their way in and out of cars and trucks that were stalled in the traffic at a long traffic light. Harry and Carly both noticed that everyone seemed to be heading to the airport, if the overhead English-Thai traffic signs were to be believed.

But now it was Carly who hurried Harry along, saying over and over again, "Wat Po! Wat Po! Krit's gotta be there! He'll know what to do. Krit will know…."

Then Carly stopped in her tracks by the oddest sight.

"Wow," she said, a little spooked, as she stood looking in the window of an airport taxi.

"Look, Harry," she said. "That kid in the taxi. He's building an airplane section with Legos. Just like Mack."

Harry wasn't sure why he was supposed to be impressed. "So he has Legos," he said. "I hate to tell you, but they have McDonalds here, too. And a Wendy's. It's a big city."

"That's not what I'm getting at," Carly sighed. "Don't you think it's strange he's building an airplane section with them, while he's driving to the airport? Who does that?"

With that, car horns honked impatiently and the scooters and tuk-tuks started to rev their engines. It was as if everyone, all bunched up at the traffic light had the collective intelligence of a colony of ants. They all leaned expectantly forward, preparing to rush headlong down the road, all-at-once, after the light flipped to green.

Carly and Harry stumbled into Wat Po, sweaty and haggard, but their hopes for a hiding place were immediately dashed. The Thai military, after all, were no fools. Wat Po was where they had found them the first time they escaped, so Wat Po was the obvious place to check after they escaped again.

"I knew this was a bad idea," Carly said, standing out among the robed monks in her bright T-shirt and sneakers.

Radios crackled to life all around them, as plain-clothed agents stationed at the entrances immediately spotted the two kids. Before Carly and Harry knew it, they were being followed, by an ever-tightening ring of men who didn't exactly look like they were there to offer smiling prayers to the Buddha.

"It's no use, Harry!" Carly said, as she realized they'd been discovered.

Harry just charged ahead trying to get back to Krit, taking his chances that something Indiana Jones-ish would happen to delay their capture: a huge runaway boulder, a wave of writhing snakes, a rope bridge dropping out of nowhere... But a quick glance at his surroundings told him this wasn't the kind of neighborhood where those things were likely to happen.

They burst through the temple entrance, and into the place where they'd met Krit before.

Sure enough, there he sat, chanting prayers in a haze of incense smoke.

He looked up in surprise, but this time worry washed across his face as his eyes darted back and forth between Carly, Harry, and the doorway they'd just come through.

"What are you two doing back here?" he asked.

"We escaped!" Harry said proudly, with a bit toothy smile.

"They were going to put us in prison for two years!" Carly added, still amazed at the cruelty of the sentence.

"Oh no," Krit said, "No jail for you two. Oh, no. The King of Thailand said many years ago that no kids go to prison here. They are all sent home. Parents worse punishment than jail for kids who do wrong."

Carly glanced over to Harry with a look that said many things at once, but mostly it said, *"Harry, are we in this awful mess because maybe you didn't know what the heck you were talking about?"*

But she didn't have time to even finish her thought. Once again, soldiers burst into Krit's temple, only this time their commander had taken no chances; he had sent a patrol that was easily double the size of the last one.

The soldiers gruffly grabbed Carly and Harry. Then, to everyone's surprise, they went for Krit, thinking that he must have had something to do with the escape. After all, this was the second time they had found the fugitives in his company.

But Krit wasn't having any of it, and the peaceful monk suddenly showed a different side than what Mack, Carly, and Harry has seen earlier that day. He made a kind of a hand signal to the other monks who watched nearby, twirled his robe to distract the soldiers, and then dashed off toward the inner sanctum of the Wat, where the soldiers were not allowed.

As the soldiers were distracted by Krit, and just as Carly and Harry were marched out of the Wat, one of the monks caught Carly's eye and made as if to throw her something—the crystal, Mack's crystal! The monk tossed it and she caught it without slowing down her step.

Great, Carly thought bitterly, *a lot of good this stupid rock has done us.* But she slipped it into her pocket anyway, before any of the soldiers could see what had happened.

Then Carly and Harry were hustled off to a waiting van. One of the soldiers spoke to them in broken English, as he tried to explain what was going to happen to them.

"You kids way too much trouble," he said. "Capture, escape, run, run, capture, escape. Pain in fanny. We have to feed you, but you eat like killer whales. We let you use phones for *long, long* distance calls. We send you home now. Too much trouble."

"What about Mack? Where's he?" Harry insisted. "We're not leaving without Mack."

"Oh, we have special flight for all you," the policeman said airily. "You would all be home now if you not run away. You supposed to go on regular flight last night. That gone now. Your friend and his papa still here, and now you all earned special places," he said, laughing.

"You all criminals now," he laughed again. "Everyone on same charter flight now. Leaving tonight. We taking you criminals to the airport now. Bye-bye, criminals!"

"Mack's Dad is here?" Carly asked. "You mean, here in Thailand?"

"Oh sure," the solider said, looking out the window, as the daily calamity of the Bangkok streets unfolded around them. "Yes, he come on private jet. Very expensive to do that. Who pays the gas? Who pays fancy hotel for pilots? Maybe you have rich mama and papa? Maybe you have credit card for that?"

He turned around to look at Harry and smiled, a single gold tooth catching the light of the tropical sun.

"Hey, don't look at me!" Harry said. "Besides, we have to get another card, because that old one is maxed out, I think."

Carly gave Harry another one of her looks.

They rode along in silence for a time, stuck in the agonizing stop-and-go traffic that crawled along at a snail's pace as they made their way back to the Bangkok airport.

Then Harry looked out the window, and this time he noticed something odd. It was not the first time he'd seen such a thing today, which made it seem only stranger.

"Hey, there's another one! Look at that kid," he said pointing, "The kid in the car next to us."

"Boy from Africa," the Thai solider said. "Yes, from Mali. You know Mali, in Africa? That's embassy car. Not strange to see that here."

"Harry, look. He's building something with Legos," Carly said. "He's got a huge Lego set, like Mack's."

"Isn't that weird?" Harry said. "That somebody with a Lego set like the one we hauled over here to Thailand should be on the way to the airport at the same time we are? And that we just saw something like that in another car?"

"Maybe," Carly said, "but stranger things have happened, Harry. Stranger things like *someone* not understanding that kids can't go to prison in Thailand, and then talking other law-abiding kids into escaping from a police station where, it turns out, we were merely waiting to fly home."

"I'm sorry," Harry said, "but what you just said was so long and boring that I must've fallen asleep for a second there."

After being stuck in traffic for close to an hour, the solider looked at his watch with worry. The last thing he wanted was to miss the assigned flight. If he had to return the kids to the police station, he'd have to spend one more night with these brats in the lock up. No way.

He muttered something to the driver, who switched on the sirens and they were off in a whirl of flashing lights. They raced through traffic, even going up on the sidewalk once to get around an elephant.

When they finally pulled up to the airport drop-off area, it was the same airport where Carly, Harry, and Mack had made their first escape, and it looked very familiar now to Carly and Harry. They had arrived in Thailand a short time ago with nearly nothing, and they were leaving with less, just the clothes on their backs and the crystal in Carly's pocket.

One of the other soldiers escorted them through the immigration area of the airport, where they bypassed security. They had no luggage to look through, anyway. They ended up in the same room where they'd been before.

"They just put us in here to wait, right? Right?" Carly asked the solider. "We're not back in prison… are we?"

But the solider didn't say anything. He probably didn't speak English anyway, she thought.

"Just for two years, that's all," Harry said, holding his head in his hands. "Do you like your new home for the next two years, Carly? Think you can dress it up a bit, maybe put some posters on the wall…?"

"No, Harry," Carly sighed. "Haven't you been listening? The man said we were on a plane tonight!"

"Yeah, probably taking us to Devil's Island."

With that the door opened and in walked Mack, Jake, and John Hannigan.

"Dudes, you're here!" Mack said. He gave high fives to Carly and Harry, as Jake McCarthy and John Hannigan looked on. Realizing that she should have said a proper hello, Carly gave Jake McCarthy a quick hug, and said, "Sorry for all the trouble, Mr. McCarthy. We… We… "

Then Harry started to speak, saving her from having to explain. "We are very, very happy to be heading home even in the economy seats, given proper access to food, Mr. McCarthy," is what Harry said in his most-polite and proper voice.

Then Mack chimed in with an angry, insistent voice, saying to his Dad and Mr. Hannigan, "We're not going home without solving the A.D. airplane situation."

"Enough of that, Mack," Jake McCarthy snapped at him, sounding frustrated. "Mack, there's nothing we can do. I told you, I tried to check A.D.'s flight, but we have no idea what plane she's on. We're just have to trust that fate has steered her to a safe flight home."

John Hannigan, who hadn't said a word, suddenly looked at his watch and seemed to snap to life. "Yikes, you all have to get going."

He shook everyone's hands goodbye, pumping Harry's hand up and down in an exaggerated way that really communicated his intense desire to get everyone out of Thailand as soon as possible.

"Well!" Hannigan said, "You've all certainly brightened up the last couple of days for me, children. And to think, all this time I could have been sitting in my air-conditioned office, making lunch plans or going to the gym. Instead, I've had the distinct pleasure of chasing after police cars and appealing to the Thai king to release American criminals who escaped not once but *twice* from his majesty's military forces."

"Oh the distinct pleasure was ours! Think nothing of it," Harry said with his new formal politeness, not understanding that Hannigan was not being serious.

"Um, Harry," Carly said, tapping him on his shoulder as Harry continued to pump his handshake with Hannigan. "I think Mr. Hannigan was kind of…you know…joking."

Carly, Mack, and Jake just threw up their hands in pretend exasperation when Harry replied, "And who ever said we weren't interested in lunch plans?"

Chapter Twenty

A Missing Number

"Jeez, what is this, a Lego convention?!" Harry said to himself when he saw more and more kids with Legos in the airport. He was making his way to the food court to see if there was (maybe? perhaps? one could only hope!) a teensy weensy bit of room to charge things on his fake credit card after all. He had grown oh so tired of Thai rice and eggs, and he wanted a good-old-fashioned American cheeseburger. Yeah, and some fries, and some American root beer to wash it all down.

After the Thai soldiers had finally released the three young adventurers into the custody of Jake McCarthy, and they had gotten through the immigration checkpoint, Harry assumed they were all free to roam around the airport. Jake wasn't exactly pleased to discover that Harry had wandered off when his back was turned, leaving Jake to hold his place in line for the plane. Worse, their flight was leaving from a remote gate down a long corridor, where only the charter flights assembled their crews and gathered up passengers.

Harry made a beeline to the food court and boldly ordered up his junk food, not even trying to use the few Thai words he'd picked up over the last few days. Somehow his credit card sailed through, prompting a loud *"Yippee!"* from Harry that attracted stares. Then he yelled across the counter, as though a louder voice would make his English more understandable: "Could you possibly make that cheeseburger a double? If it's too late to change the order, I understand, but how much work is it really to throw another patty on the grill with a slice of cheese?"

The burger arrived. Harry was alive with glee.

Then the mountain of fries came soon after that, served up in a bucket large enough to be a trash can, along with an equally large soda that Harry watched with delight as it sloshed its way across the counter and into his hungry hands.

Harry couldn't have been more pleased, as he gathered up his meal and chowed on down, while taking joy rides on one of the airport's moving sidewalks. It was during his fourth round-trip, moving-sidewalk excursion when he saw, coming the other direction on the neighboring moving sidewalk, someone who looked very familiar. But he just couldn't place her face.

The two approached each other, as Harry continued to stuff his face as fast as he could. The long-braided woman in the different-colored sneakers noticed Harry and stared just as intently as him, trying to place *his* face. She had this feeling that she knew him, but after all, the last person she expected to see in the Bangkok airport was a neighborhood friend of Mack's.

As the moving sidewalk swept them along and they drifted nearer, their eyes locked; they stared at each other with vague smiles on their faces.

Then, just as Harry was about to get off his end of the moving sidewalk, and just as A.D. was about to get off her end, they both spun around and yelled out each other's name.

"*A.D.!*"

"*Harry!*"

A.D. rushed back to talk to Harry, with a quizzical smile on her face.

"Harry! What in the name of the Great Sleeping Buddha are you doing here?" she said.

"You're A.D., Mack's aunt, right?" Harry said, just to make sure. He'd only met her once, when she nearly ran him down while backing out of Mack's driveway.

"Yes, of course it's me," she said. "What are doing in Thailand?"

"Duh, we came looking for you!" he said, as if she should have known.

"We? Who is *we?*" A.D. asked with an incredulous laugh.

"Me, and Mack…" Harry started to say before she cut him off.

"Mack's here? In Thailand?"

"And Carly and Mack's dad…" Harry continued.

"Are you serious? All here? And you've been looking for me the entire time?"

"Yes, except when we were in jail… or escaping from jail, you know, running from soldiers," Harry said.

"Jail?! You went to jail?"

"Two jails, actually," Harry said between French fries, as if it were nothing special.

A.D. stood there amazed, trying to understand what Harry was saying. "And Jake, Mack's dad, was he in jail too?"

"Oh yes," Harry said.

A.D.'s hand flew to her mouth.

"Not for long, though, just for a visit," Harry explained. "He flew over in a private jet to get us out of the slammer."

A.D. stood in stunned silence, wondering what to believe. But then the moment was made even more odd when two young boys walked past, comparing their Lego structures, trying to fit their two assemblies together.

"Wow, that's weird, isn't it?" A.D. said. "Kids in Thailand playing Legos like that."

"Well," Harry said, "ordinarily I'd agree with you, but I've seen it too many times today to be surprised."

"Me too!" A.D. said, looking up a bit mystified, as she thought back to the boys she'd seen assembling Legos on her bus, and then in the bus that passed in the lane next to her.

"When we were in traffic earlier," Harry said, "we saw other kids with Legos on their way to the airport."

With all the talk about jail and Legos, A.D. and Harry lost track of time, until they were interrupted by an urgent loudspeaker announcement: *"Last call for boarding charter flight 652 to Washington, D.C. All passengers should be on board at this time at gate 57-50."*

Looking mildly panicked, Harry and A.D. sprinted to the gate. They were just about the last people walking down the jetway when they heard a booming voice shout: "A.D.!"

It was Jake, along with Mack and Carly as they stood in the doorway of the jet.

"I can't believe it!" Jake said, genuinely astonished. "You're on this flight? *Our* flight? You can't believe how hard I've looked to find you. I've practically had the entire U.S. government on the job, and you waltz in here as though you're coming back from a stroll around the block."

A.D. was almost too amazed to speak. "I can't believe you're in Thailand. Harry was just telling me about the… being in… It's sooo… I mean, what are you all doing here?"

But at this point, the flight steward had had just about enough of this cozy family get-together, and he waved his arms wildly, as though he was herding birds, to get everyone on board to find their seats.

"Come on, folks," he said. "Save the family reunion for thirty-five thousand feet, please. We have to get this plane off the ground."

A.D. and the kids moved inside the fuselage, but Jake lingered near the doorway, his attention captivated by something very strange. A.D. stopped and looked back.

"Jake," she said, "did you forget something?"

Actually, she thought he looked more alarmed than forgetful, but he broke out of his momentary trance and went to find his seat.

"No… no…" Jake said, "I must have just zoned out there for a minute. Too many times zones in the last 24 hours. Jet lag…"

Back at their seats, Carly leaned over and spoke in a surprised half-whisper to Harry, "Did you see that?"

"What?" Harry asked.

"Other side of the aisle, one row up. Those two kids, the ones with the Legos. They have crystals, too, just like Mack's!"

"I know!," Harry said. "I saw two *other* kids with Legos in the front of the plane, and they both had rose crystals."

Carly was speechless for a long moment.

"Hey, you think they came from that same cave where Evers got his crystal?" Harry asked, standing up a bit to get a better look. "The crystals look kinda the same."

"I don't know," Carly said, "I'm really creeped out by the fact that all these kids with crystals and Legos all somehow ended up on our plane."

She reached into her pocket, just to check to make sure… Good, Mack's crystal was still there.

Back at his seat, Mack had just sat down, but then he looked up to see Jake and A.D. getting out of their seats and walking back up to the door of the plane. Jake seemed to be looking around the doorway again. Then A.D. pointed to something nearby that Jake briefly checked out, only to shake his head *no*.

The suspense was killing Mack. He unbuckled his seat belt and walked back to see what they were talking about.

But now the flight steward had reached the limit of his patience, which even on good days was pretty low. After all, he had *specifically* told everyone to remain buckled – like that man and that lady in the different-colored shoes examining the doorway for some cockamamie reason. Nothing got under his skin more than passengers who ignored regulations.

Stay calm, he told himself. Taking a deep breath, the steward picked up the microphone and made his announcement:

"Will everyone please return to your seats. The plane cannot take off if people are up and about… Yes, that's you, sir… and you, ma'am… With the freaky sneakers. Yes. Will everyone… Hello…? Everyone *please* take their seats! Please! We're not here to play musical chairs, folks, this is an international flight and certain rules apply, and they apply to everyone!"

A.D., Mack, and Jake all hurried for their seats, but something was *still* bothering Jake. Risking another scolding from the steward, he got up again and hurried up to the jet doorway before they closed the hatch. This time he took a penlight from his pocket and scanned the area just over the doorway. Suddenly – he spotted something and he froze. Sure enough – his eyes weren't fooling him after all – there was the serial number plate attached above the doorway, but the serial number had been partially scratched out.

For just an instant, Jake was paralyzed with fear. But then he also realized that lots of passenger's eyes were on him, including Carly, Harry, A.D., and Mack's. They were wondering the same thing: What could be drawing worried attention from America's top crash site investigator. Even worse, what could make someone like that freeze for a second in fear.

Another pair of eyes were on him too. The steward's. He was in the back of the cabin and hadn't seen Jake get up from his seat for the third time. Until now. He smacked his head in disbelief, as he looked at Jake, and then rushed up the aisle to confront him, mouthing the words *"I can't believe it!"* – over and over again.

Chapter Twenty-One

A Lurch

The 747 rolled smoothly onto the runway. As Jake buckled into his seat, he told A.D. that a full explanation of why he and the kids were in Thailand would just have to wait until they were fully airborne.

Of course, A.D. was very eager to hear the full story, but Jake seemed a little… preoccupied at the moment. She already had a nagging feeling that something very unusual was happening on the plane. And it wasn't just that Jake was acting freaky. A remarkable number of boys and girls on the flight were wearing crystals and assembling Legos. What could it mean?

Before A.D. could say anything more, Carly leaned over and said to her, "Are you seeing what I'm seeing, A.D.?"

"The Legos?" A.D. asked with a forced smile that tried to mask a deeper worry.

"Like duh, A.D.," Carly said with a laugh. "But look, everyone with a Lego has some kind of rose crystal. Everyone. I didn't notice it at first, because they're not all holding them in their hands. Some are wearing them as necklaces, rings, bracelets, and one kid has his crystal set in his belt buckle."

A.D. looked at Carly in bewilderment. A.D. suddenly seemed transfixed with a kind of awe. She didn't understand the whys and wherefores, but she knew she was encountering something that was truly unexplainable.

"Assembled," A.D. said softly to no one and everyone at the same time, her face lit with an almost saintly glow. "We've been assembled here."

"What?" Carly said, with a catch in her voice. The spooky look on A.D.'s face frightened her a little.

"'Assembled'?" Carly asked, "What do you mean?"

"We've all been gathered here, don't you see? On this flight. These kids. These people. With all these powers, we're here to keep the order of things," A.D. said, sweeping her arms broadly, as a peaceful smile washed across her face. "These holders of the crystals... and us. We're here on purpose, Carly. It's no accident we're on this plane."

A.D. looked over to Jake and Mack, but their faces were buried in papers, as Jake frantically shuffled from page to page and Mack hovered with a pen in one hand and a notebook in the other, furiously taking notes.

A.D. looked to Harry, only to catch the tail end of what he was saying to the flight attendant.

"... that's a large Coke with extra ice, and if I could have a few bags of those delectable-looking pretzels we saw on the way in, I'd be forever grateful."

A.D. just laughed as the plane moved closer to the runway for takeoff.

Then, very quickly, and as smooth as silk, the plane lifted off into the skies above Thailand.

It climbed at a steep angle as the jet engines roared, but then suddenly, there was a huge *boom!* with the sound of metal-on-metal… and breaking glass.

Jake looked up in a frightened panic. Mack, too. Carly clutched A.D.'s hand and squeezed.

But it wasn't the plane that made the noise after all. A rolling drink service cart had broken loose from its latch, and it was sailing down the aisle, gaining speed, with no one to stop it.

Harry reached his hand out, as Jake yelled, "No, Harry, don't! It'll rip your arm off! Let it go!" But Harry had no intention of trying to stop the cart. As it whizzed by, he simply reached out and, with perfect timing, snatched several bags of peanuts from the top tray, which he then tossed to everyone around him in two seconds flat. Harry was eyeing his prize as the cart careened to the back of the plane, where the steward finally stopped it.

"The good lord seems to be throwing things directly at me now," the beleaguered steward said to no one.

But Harry and the peanut-bag incident were highly entertaining, and it somehow broke the tension. Jake and A.D. finally relaxed a bit and let out a big laugh, which made Mack and Carly laugh, as Harry just looked up and said defensively, "Hey, sue me, I like peanuts!"

It was then that Carly took the time to fill in A.D. on all their travels, reaching all the way back – it seemed like years ago, not just a few days – to the limo driver, the pilfered cell phones, and Harry's highly questionable credit card. She told A.D. about how the Thai soldiers had pulled them off the plane, and how they ended up running into Krit on the streets of Bangkok, how he led them to Wat Po, and how he seemed to even recognize Mack, and how they got captured and re-captured by the soldiers.

"But wait a minute," A.D. said, "I'm getting all the details, but not the overall picture. Why did you come over here in the first place?"

"Oh, I thought Jake told you," Carly said in surprise. "We were trying to stop you from getting on a bad airplane, the lemon that keeps showing up as a charter plane. Mack's Dad tracked the numbers as far as he could. At first, it looked like you were in real trouble. But now that you were switched to this plane with us, everything's fine. Right? I just hope the people on that plane you were supposed to be on will be all – "

A.D. interrupted, "Hold it, Carly, I never switched planes. This is the same charter flight I was always booked on."

A cold chill ran down Carly's back.

Even Harry, who was barely listening in, stopped eating long enough to listen to what A.D. was saying.

With that, the announcement chimes rang out and the pilot came on the loudspeaker to say that they had now reached an altitude of thirty-five thousand feet, and it was safe to move about the cabin.

With a sheaf of papers in one hand, Jake got up and walked quickly to the midsection of the plane. He opened the bathroom door, but instead of going inside, he examined a label on the door. There he saw one more reason to be afraid: The plane's serial number was partially scratched out there, too. He could make out only the first three numbers: 171. Sensing someone was watching him, Jake wheeled around, and there was A.D. standing over him.

"Jake," she said in a quiet voice, "I beg you to tell me what's going on?"

Before answering, he cast a quick look around to make sure they wouldn't be overheard. "Did you switch planes, or was this the charter you were originally scheduled to be on?"

"No. I was just telling Carly, this is the same flight, same ticket I've always had."

"A.D., I'm afraid that this is the plane we've been looking for all along…"

"The lemon? The bad plane?" she asked.

"Yeah," Jake said. Then he did a double-take. "Wait, how did you know about the lemon?"

"Carly just told me."

Then Jake fatefully pointed to the partially scratched-out serial number on the restroom door. Only the first three numbers were visible.

"See that, 171?" he said. Then he pointed to his NTSB records and showed A.D. the highlighted number of the bad plane: 171-25R-056-02.

"Okay, but it's just the first three numbers that match," she said. "What are the chances…"

Jake held up a "hold that thought" finger and led A.D. over to the main plane doorway, where he first noticed the scratched out serial numbers. "But look here," he told A.D. Here the *last* three numbers are visible here."

A.D. slipped on her glasses to see better. She read "6-02."

Jake fatefully held up the NTSB records for her to see the last three numbers on the doomed plane's serial number.

6-02.

A.D. and Jake just looked at each other for a moment, before the steward rushed over to them and said: "I'm sorry, but you two have been acting funny since before this plane took off, and now, I've had it. I am warning you that I will be calling the authorities if you don't immediately get to your seats."

Jake reached into his pocket, spun around, and pulled out his NTSB crash investigator's badge.

Jake held his badge up to the steward's face, much too close at first, just to intimidate him. Then he pulled it back so the steward could read it.

"U.S. Federal Agent Jake McCarthy, NTSB investigator," Jake said.

The steward backed down, as Jake began to explain, "Unfortunately, this plane we are in…"

But Jake chose not to finish his sentence. He looked up to see that everyone in the whole back section of the plane was leaning forward, listening, hanging on to Jake's every word, including the dozen or so crystal kids who had been eagerly working on their Legos.

Jake tried to force a friendly smile so no one would get alarmed, as he pulled the steward in close to him and said in a fierce whisper: *"Can we immediately meet with the pilot? We are in imminent danger."*

Chapter Twenty-Two

Crystals Everywhere

The steward was wide-eyed with astonishment at who Jake McCarthy claimed to be. He checked Jake's NTSB badge one more time, just to make sure this wasn't an elaborate terrorist hoax. Then he and Jake headed toward the cockpit, with A.D. in tow. As they walked up the aisle, Jake saw for the first time the unlikely sight that Harry, A.D., Carly, and Mack had all reported earlier: There were a few kids… no, several kids – Jake swallowed hard as he fully took in what his eyes had up to now refused to see – there were *a lot* of kids on board who were busily working on Legos.

"Are we, uh, headed to a Lego convention or something?" he asked the steward.

But A.D. interrupted, whispering "Look closer, Jake. They've all got rose crystals."

It was true, he noticed. All the Lego-playing kids seemed to have crystals worn as rings, necklaces, or just loose like Mack's.

"Where's yours?" Jake asked A.D. "Didn't you put it back in the monastery cave?"

"Believe me, I tried to," A.D. started to say, looking like she wanted to tell a longer version of the story when they had more time with fewer distractions.

"You tried? What do you mean? All you had to do was leave it there and walk away, right?" Once again, Jake found himself stubbornly clinging to his shaky belief that Mack's crystal was in no way special.

"Jake, I tried, believe me. I left it there. I did," A.D. said with a sigh, "but when I got on the plane today, it... just reappeared. Here it is." A.D. reached into her backpack and pulled out her half of Evers' crystal.

It was all too much for Jake to understand. But crystals were not his most pressing concern. So he marched up the aisle to the cockpit.

He didn't get far.

Everyone on board heard another loud boom, but this time it wasn't a drink cart. The plane started to shake violently.

People screamed.

Panic rippled through the plane. There was something funny going on. Something not quite... right. You could just feel it in the air.

Suddenly, Jack and A.D. crouched low to keep from being knocked over by the force of the violent shaking. The steward hustled back to the P.A. system and started to appeal for calm, as overhead storage bins popped open.

The plane started to rapidly lose altitude.

With a half crouch, half run, Jake made it to the cockpit and banged on the security door.

"NTSB. Permission to enter place," he said.

Then he had to yell it again over the loud whistling sound that began to fill the cabin. Following standard procedure, he held his badge up to the small security window in the cockpit door.

The cockpit door swung open to reveal two pilots and a navigator, all looking mystified as they stared at a cockpit full of gauges.

"I'm Jake McCarthy, Federal Crash Investigator," he said. "What have you got?"

"What have we got?" the pilot shouted back in frustration. His I.D. badge identified him as Will Sheppard, and he wore Air Force veteran patches on his flight uniform. Obviously a seasoned professional, Jake thought, maybe even an air combat veteran.

"What we've got, Agent McCarthy," Capitan Sheppard went on, "what we've got is a 747 unexpectedly out of control and losing attitude at a rate that'll have us in an uncontrolled landing in thirty-two minutes. That's what we got!"

Jake studied the gauges as Captain Sheppard worked the wing controls to try to slow the descent. He drew back on the thrust from the engines – a necessary precaution, Jake knew, because even though the plane was sinking, it seemed to be traveling forward at a high rate of speed.

"What's the nearest runway where we can land?" Jake asked.

"That's the problem," the co-pilot Dee Logan said with a sigh. He was younger man than the pilot, and his nervousness betrayed his relative inexperience in crisis situations. "It's five hundred miles away. We've got to fly this plane on our own and keep it in the air, or we're going to crash it in the ocean. There's no half-way point between those two options."

Someone tapped Jake on his shoulder to get his attention. He didn't turn around to see who it was. He just called out, "Not now."

But the tapping continued until Jake spun around, ready to chew someone's head off.

But it was A.D. and she stood there, calmly smiling.

"Jake, you gotta see this," she said, and pointed back to the passenger section of the plane.

Jake glanced to the back section of the plane, just to quiet her. But then, the sight he saw wouldn't let him look away. To his astonishment, all the crystal kids were gathered in the center aisle –some working alone, and some working in teams – madly assembling airplane sections with their Legos. They worked from a large single pile of Lego pieces on the floor, which they had all contributed to from their own supply.

One person was clearly in charge of the effort, and it was Mack. He moved quickly from kid to kid and team to team, while Carly and Harry – each with a red marker in hand – kept a running status record of each mini-Lego project by writing on the very wall of the plane.

Kids out of their seats during turbulence…blocking the aisles… writing on the walls with red markers… The steward is going to lose it for sure, Jake thought.

Leaving the confused cockpit behind, Jake and A.D. walked back to watch in stunned silence as Mack spoke in a commanding voice to the entire group of kids: "Who's working on the tail section? Please state your names."

Two hands shot up, as the twin boys from Thailand spoke in turn:

"See!"

"Kwan!"

They said their next words together, as though it were rehearsed and planned: "We'll take the tail section."

Kwan wore his rose crystal on a chain around his neck. As he leaned forward it caught the sun, sending rays of light streaming in through the plane's west-facing windows. For an instant, a rose-tinted rainbow washed across the inside of the entire plane.

"And who's got the wings?" Mack yelled. The boy from Mali, who Harry and Carly had seen in Bangkok traffic, raised his hand.

"Mali!" he cried out.

"That's where you're from, Mack said. "But what's your name?"

"Mali," he said again, mildly annoyed. "The wings are all mine. Oh, do I ever love making wings!"

"Save it for the airport lounge," Harry shot back.

"Central fuselage?" Mack demanded, as the 747 rolled a bit to the left, provoking several shouts and groans from the passengers before stabilizing. "Who's on it?"

"Over here," came a shout. "Rhajimi!"

"Noorda!"

The two Indian girls with matching rose crystal rings amazingly had the fuselage already nearly finished, because – as they told an amazed Mack – they had somehow *known* to work on the fuselage before the plane was even in trouble.

"Great," Mack yelled, clenching his fists in triumph at the progress they were making, even as the plane sank lower and lower in the sky.

For each section of the plane that Mack needed to be built from Legos, all he had to do was yell out a section by name, and volunteers' hands shot into the air. Immediately teams were assigned, as they promptly set to work.

"Forward landing gear!" Mack yelled. An especially mysterious team of two boys claimed the job. It wasn't exactly time to be overly selective about who worked on what part of the plane, or even to stop and think about it, but even Mack and A.D. had to pause a second to stare at these boys, whose faces no one could really see, because they both wore exotic bejeweled cloaks across their heads and faces.

"All yours, mystery boys," Mack said in an I-don't-wanna-know-about it voice, "All yours…"

"Status on under-wing landing gear?" Carly shouted out, her red marker poised in her hand, as she kept notes. Kids gave her their reports.

"Under-wing landing gear!" Mack yelled, re-focusing on the task at hand. "Who's on it?"

"Already complete, Mack," said an American boy named Dean Blaise. Remarkably, Dean had also been compelled to work on that project in advance. He too had begun building his under-wing landing gear Lego long before the plane was even in trouble. He had dreamed about it for two weeks, he later told Mack.

"Listen up," Mack shouted. "We have to fit all these sections together, and see what's working and what's not. And we haven't got much time."

Two rows down from where Jake stood marveling at this sight, , he overheard one old retiree say in exasperation to his silver-haired wife: "That's it. This is the *last time* we fly charter."

"Cockpit!" Mack yelled. "Cockpit? Who's got it?" No one answered.

"I think that's yours, Mack," Harry shouted back. "Can you do it?"

"But Krit has my crystal!" Mack said.

"Oh no, he doesn't," Carly said with a grin, pulling Mack's crystal out of her pocket.

"Where did you get that?" Mack said in astonishment. I can't seem to get rid of that thing!"

"You don't want to get rid of that crystal," Harry said, as he grabbed it and joined it with A.D.'s half, which she had just passed to him. Mack grabbed the unified crystal and started in, as if trying to extract power from it. After five seconds of focused silence, he began frantically assembling Lego pieces for the cockpit.

The 747 rolled again, but even as it sank lower, it seemed to be pointing upward – dangerous combination.

Jake yelled to the pilot in the real cockpit: "Can you give it more thrust?" But the captain shook his head and yelled back, "We're at maximum allowable speed already, and I'm only at one-quarter throttle. I'm trying to pull this bird up, but it won't climb!"

Piece by piece, the various teams of kids hurried to complete the assembly of their 747 sections, all hoping that each piece would eventually fit together… and maybe save their own lives by telling them what was wrong with the plane.

"As you assemble your sections," Mack instructed his teams, "every little detail matters. If it doesn't fit together, there's a reason for that. Don't forget: Any mismatch could be the root of the problem with the plane. So don't force your pieces. Pay attention."

The kids all worked like mad, heroically ignoring the fact that they were twenty minutes away from crashing.

"Uh, what exactly are these kids doing, may I ask?" the steward asked Jake, casting a doubtful glare at what *had* to be against flight regulations. He was just about to force everyone back into their seats for safety, when Jake stopped him.

"They're solving the crash before it happens," he said. "As far as I can tell, it works every time."

"Oh won't *this* make a great movie some day," the steward murmured with rolling eyes.

Still, Jake kept a watchful eye out the window as the plane dropped through the twenty-thousand foot cloud cover.

"Every time, Dad?" Mack questioned, reminding his father that they didn't exactly have a perfect track record solving crashes.

With that, Jake winked at the steward, saying, "Well, *almost* every time. Let's hope we're lucky and the team of kids we've got on this flight is strong enough when working together. There's no way that just one of them could solve this working alone."

"Solve what?" the steward asked, still mystified as to what was going on. But the energy of the Lego teams, along with Jake's confidence, overwhelmed the steward's doubts, and he just stood by and watched.

Watching the kids work was like watching industrious bees, where each bee works on one section of its hive, oblivious to the larger design, only to look up and discover they've created a magnificent architectural miracle.

Then, as all the passengers watched in fascination, the Lego model plane started to come together before their very eyes. Piece by piece, and section by section, the kids created a stunningly accurate replica of the 747. It was happening so fast, it was almost as though the model were being assembled by a force from beyond.

All the kids' fingers worked nimbly and furiously, as though somehow guided. Rhajmi and Noorda, the two girls from India, even worked part of the time with their eyes closed.

"How can you do that?" Harry said, as he rolled up the drink cart and distributed ice cream bars.

"Goes much faster when you're not looking," Rhajmi said.

"This way, you're not second-guessing yourself," Noorda added.

"Oh, sure, me too! Watch this," Harry said, closing his eyes to expertly unwrap a Klondike Bar.

Mack worked just as furiously, adding Lego piece after Lego piece. He also made magically fast progress on the cockpit assembly.

Then he was ready for the next step, the big step, and all the kids seemed anxiously ready as well.

"Ok, let's bring the sections together!" Mack shouted, as the teams lifted their sections into the air.

A loud collective *Ahhh!* went up from everyone in the plane. The passengers had watched in both amazement and bewilderment as the kids had worked furiously on what some, at first, considered just an annoying pile of Legos that blocked the path to the bathroom…but which then morphed into a magnificent and eerily accurate replica of the very plane they were all sitting in.

And if there ever was a sight to go *Ahhh!* about, everyone agreed, this was it. Once the sections were all assembled, they made a model ten feet long… and the detail was *amazing!* Right down to the airplane windows. One older woman got out of her seat and picked out the window on the

Lego model that corresponded to the window she was sitting next to on the plane. She looked inside the tiny window, half expecting to see a miniature version of herself staring back.

"Tail section first!" Mack called out, as kids presented their completed work.

"Careful, careful!" Mack commanded, even as the real 747 pitched forward, and then rolled from side to side.

"Steady guys!" Jake yelled up to the cockpit. "Can you buy us some time? Even a few minutes?" But the pilot and co-pilot were still only vaguely aware of what was going on in the back of the plane. They had assumed, without being told, that it was some crazy activity meant to distract everyone before the plane went down.

"Wings!" Mack yelled as he continued to snap together the sections to create a unified model.

Jake McCarthy looked on, but as the frontal section of the fuselage was assembled, he noticed a piece on the model that wasn't on the 747 they were flying in.

Mack saw the same thing at the same time, and Jake caught Mack's eye with a quizzical look. Then Jake pointed to a spot on the outside of the plane near the emergency exit door, before pointing to the same place on the model.

Mack continued frantically assembling the model 747, as Jake shouted to the once-suspicious steward, who now was too wowed by what the kids were doing to interfere.

"Steward," Jake yelled. *"Steward!"* he yelled again to snap him out his trance. "Check our airspeed with the captain and ask him what his indicators are saying."

The steward hurried off to the cockpit and immediately yelled back: "The airspeed indicators are pinned on maximum. We're flying at the top speed allowed for this airplane. And he's still at one-quarter throttle."

Jake and Mack looked at the Lego model, where two airspeed probes were in their proper positions right above the wings. Then they both looked out the window and saw something that made them immediately realize what was wrong with the plane. It was just what they had suspected a minute ago.

"The airspeed sensors are gone! They've been removed!" Mack said.

"The pilot says we're at maximum speed," Jake yelled. "But it's a phantom reading. The gauges are giving wrong readings."

Mack and Jake looked at each other and whooped and hollered. Then they said the same thing at the same time: *"He doesn't know it, but we're flying too slow!"*

Jake and Mack both ran to the cockpit, even as the plane shook in turbulence, plunging down through the 10,000 foot level, and sinking fast.

Jake burst through the cockpit entrance, with Mack right behind him. "Your airspeed indicators are faulty!" Jake shouted.

"We're flying too slow!" Mack said.

Then Captain Will Sheppard and his co-pilot Dee spun around in stunned disbelief. Sheppard tapped the dials that showed how fast they were going, but the gauge didn't move.

"It seems like we're getting consistent readings," he told Jake. "I'm sorry, McCarthy, but I don't believe you. I *can't* believe you. I've got to stick by my instruments," Sheppard said.

Mack begged the pilot to come with him and Jake to the back of the plane.

Sheppard protested at first. "I'm the pilot of an airplane in an uncontrolled descent! I can't leave the cockpit," he said.

"Please," Mack said, and the look on Mack's face – half-pleading, half as calm as the face of the Sleeping Buddha – finally made the pilot relent. "All right, all right, I'll come take a look. After all," Sheppard said, "What do we got to lose, but three hundred lives and a sixty-five million-dollar aircraft?"

Mack, Jake, and Sheppard all raced to the back of the plane where the kids were working.

"Where are the airspeed sensors supposed to be?" Mack knowingly asked, as he pointed to the model the crystal kids had assembled. But the pilot was speechless, astonished at what he was looking at: A perfect scale model of a 747 made entirely of Legos. Even though the real 747 was moving down through 9,000 feet, on its way to a crash landing, Captain Sheppard was momentarily hypnotized by the sight. He ran his hands over the surface of the Lego plane, his eyes almost glassy in disbelief.

He managed to mumble a few words out: "How…? How have you…? I mean, what is this? How could you have made this so quickly…?"

Now a computer voice could be heard announcing the plane's altitude over the P.A. system: *"Passing through eight thousand feet..."*

"The air speed sensors," the pilot said, snapping back into reality. "Well, they're right here, where they're supposed to be," he said, pointing to the highly accurate Lego assembly.

"Passing through seven thousand feet…" the P.A. system barked out.

"But look outside the window," Mack said, "they're missing on the plane. The sensors have been removed!"

The pilot raced over to the window and looked out, and he too quickly understood what Jake and Mack already knew. All three of them said the same thing at the same time, this time joined by all the kids who had worked on the model, as well as some of the passengers who had been hanging on every word. The way everyone almost sang it out, it sounded almost like a playground chant or a nursery rhyme: *"We're flying too slow!"*

Captain Sheppard sprinted toward the cockpit as the P.A. system announced, *"Passing through six thousand feet…"*

The pilot started yelling to Dee, his co-pilot before he was even back in the cockpit: "Full throttle and aim the nose down!"

"Full throttle, sir?" Dee questioned. "Aim it down? You sure?"

A sudden cockpit autopilot announcement underscored the confusion: *"Pull up,"* the computer voice said in an eerily authoritative voice: *"Pull up! Pull up! Fatal Error! Pull up!"*

"Turn off that worthless video game and yank the speaker wire," Captain Sheppard ordered. "We've got a faulty airspeed sensor, and we're probably going around 90 miles per hour, not 650 miles per hour. Aiming down will give us air velocity over our wings, so we can get some control back. Now, what's our altitude?"

The co-pilot's voice cracked a little in fear, as he read out the numbers: "3,500 feet, sir, and descending."

Captain Will Sheppard had to use two hands to push the throttle forward, as he yelled more instructions to his co-pilot: "Ignore the gauges! Assume they're wrong. This plane's been hot-wired, son! Now I'm going to fly it like I used to fly my old Boeing-Stearman crop duster back in Vermont!"

Sheppard defiantly went against all the cold, hard evidence right in front of him: an airspeed gauge that wrongly said they were going 650 miles per hour... the surface of the blue ocean rushing up toward them in the cockpit window, and most of all, that a twelve-year-old boy named Mack McCarthy was leading some kind of mystical team of crystal-carrying kiddies to create a Lego model that *precisely* predicted what was wrong with an airplane controlled by the most advanced aviation computers in the world!

"Promise me you'll never tell anyone about this, Dee? About how the kids with crystals had to come to our rescue?" Sheppard said, half joking. "If anyone else hears about this, there will be men in white coats waiting for me on the tarmac as soon as we land."

"That's a deal, Captain" Dee Logan said.

Sheppard plunged the throttle farther forward, and aimed the plane's nose down. Sure enough, the plane instantly responded. The plane's air speed picked up. The pilot felt the responsiveness and control return to the wings, as the co-pilot and the computer voice simultaneously counted down the altitude:

2,500 feet…

2,000 feet…

1,500 feet and 33 seconds for crash landing…

1,000 feet…

500 feet…

250 feet…

But then the numbers started to get bigger again, as the 747 finally climbed, with all four engines roaring.

"We're climbing! We're climbing!" the co-pilot cried, more surprised than relieved.

Mack and Jake stood in the cockpit door and watched a small camera out of the corner of their eye that showed the view from rear of the plane. As the plane finally gained thrust and began to climb, it was so close to the ocean surface that the air streaming out of the engines actually made a rooster-tail waterspout.

The plane finally soared, and the only thing louder than the roaring engines was the roar of the passengers, as they cheered on their crystal-wearing Lego-building heroes. They were, finally, miraculously, *safe*.

Chapter Twenty-Three

A Museum Piece

"I just love that statue of me. They captured my face perfectly," Harry said as he looked over the new Smithsonian Air and Space exhibit for the first time. "Perfect profile. You're pretty good too, Carly. And they got A.D's sneakers. Cool."

What Harry was looking at was not just a statue of himself alone. Mack, Carly, A.D., Jake, Will Sheppard, even the flight steward were all depicted in the life-sized models of the Smithsonian exhibit. The very-life-like models stood in the equally life-like aisles of the 747 that the Smithsonian experts had recreated using a few of the actual seats they had removed from the doomed 747 that the kids saved. There were models of See and Kwan. The Smithsonian model-makers did an especially good job depicting Rhajmi and Noorda, whose poses show them all working frantically in the moments before the crash was averted. In fact, many of the expressions on the models' faces seemed to capture in a freeze-frame moment the *exact instant* the kids realized they had solved the puzzle of why the plane was about to crash.

Now everyone who had been on that fateful flight a month earlier (and especially the kids, whom *USA Today* dubbed "The Little Lego Mystics," and *Time* magazine called "The

Legomaniacs") had been invited to the Smithsonian exhibit to preview it before it opened to the public.

Kwan and See were there in person, having made a return trip from Thailand. Mali had come from Mali (a fun-fact that Harry never tired of repeating: Mali from Mali, he said to anyone who would listen. Dean Blaise had come from just around the corner, where he lived. In fact, he'd skateboarded over by himself.

The centerpiece of the exhibit was, of course, the actual ten-foot Lego 747 model that had been assembled on board the plane, saving three hundred lives. A month ago, Mr. Tom Bates, a curator with the Smithsonian's Air and Space Museum, had reached Jake's cell phone just as the 747 had touched down, after it was diverted to Washington, D.C. for security reasons. Even before they had landed, the mysterious story of how the kids had saved the flight was already on news web pages all over the world. Now, Bates was calling to plead with Jake not to break up the Lego model.

"I'll try to keep it together," Jake had said, barely able to contain a smile, as he looked around at all the kids pawing at the 747 model sitting in the aisle beside him.

"You'll *try?*" Bates asked in exasperation and disbelief. "May I remind you that this is the Smithsonian's Air and Space Museum making a direct request? Did Lindbergh say, 'I'll try' when we asked him to donate the *Spirit of St. Louis.* Did NASA say 'We'll try,' when asked for the Space Shuttle?"

At this point Jake gently interrupted Bates to explain why he couldn't make promises, even to the Smithsonian.

"You see, Mr. Bates," he said, "the kids are already eyeing some rare pieces that ended up in the 747 model. They want them for their own Lego sets. Some pieces are so rare that, well, no one has ever seen them before. No one even remembers them from any of their personal collections. It's a mystery how those pieces even got on board with us."

That only made Mr. Bates want the Lego model even more.

"I beg you, Mr. McCarthy, for the sake of history and the future of aeronautical safety *and my job,*" he pleaded, "don't break up the model. Now, Jake – can I call you Jake? – let me also add that I have been in touch with the Lego company, and they are prepared to offer the crystal kids an extraordinary collection to each and every one of them: their entire inventory line, robotics sets, video games, board games, you name it. That's essentially a life-time supply of everything Lego, all in exchange for the donation of their creation to the Smithsonian. And may I also add that Lego engineers are working on an extremely limited-edition 747 kit just for the kids, but it won't be ready for a month's time."

Mr. Bates paused to take several deep breaths before concluding: "Besides walking on water, Mr. McCarthy, I don't think I can offer much more! Hello? Is the line dead? Does free toys mean anything any more? Anybody? Truckloads of free toys? Has the world gone nuts? Hello? "

Jake just looked and smiled at the kids and A.D., who had already gathered around when Jake put Bates' call on speaker phone.

"So what do you say, guys? Do we donate it to the museum?" Jake asked.

A cheer went up, of course, and the kids all agreed to do the patriotic thing and donate their creation to the world's top museum. The Lego freebies were a nice bonus, and who were they, after all, to be so rude as to turn down such a generous offer from Lego?

And now, one month after that phone call, Harry stood looking over the resulting exhibit.

"They seem to have captured everything very accurately," Harry's father, Todd Price said stiffly, as he looked on, one hand awkwardly resting on Harry's shoulder. "They even got the snack bag and soda you were determined to carry to the ocean floor if you'd crashed."

Mack and Carly tried to ignore Mr. Price, who had been saying jerky things to Harry all afternoon. It crossed both of their minds that he could at least pat Harry on the back just once and say, "Good job, son," or something like that.

"We couldn't have saved the plane without Harry," Jake said to Todd, trying to ease the tension that everyone felt.

"That's right," Lily added. "Harry was a key player in getting the right people organized on the flight. What looked like a series of rash decisions actually looks pretty smart now, wouldn't you say?"

Price realized he probably should say something nice and was just about to do so, when a familiar voice boomed from behind them all. It was the flight steward.

"Is that me? Is that my statue?" he asked, quizzing a passing visitor who he'd mistaken for the museum director. "Well, it's unacceptable. I look fearful – panicked! It's unfair, given how I was a hero in my own right, saving the flight from mass panic! I *tried* to keep everyone in their seats, but would they listen? *Oh no-o-o-o....* Who's responsible for this?"

And then the steward went off in search of a higher authority, dragging his overstuffed carry-on suitcase on wheels behind him.

All of those gathered, including A.D., Mack, and Carly, erupted in laughter. The steward was mobbed by the other kids from the flight, who pretended to mug him as they grabbed at his luggage, which toppled over and burst open to reveal what looked like—yes, it was!—gorgeous, hand-made model 747s, courtesy of the airline.

"It's the least they could do for almost killing all of us," the hapless steward murmured as he handed them out. "Well, that and first-class upgrades for life, but don't hold your breath. It is, after all, still a charter airline."

Mack and Carly just looked on confidently and quietly, as they strolled together over to look at two side exhibits, one where A.D. solemnly looked on, and another where Jake and Lily stood reading a placard. Jake started to read the words out loud, as if he were reading a news bulletin.

"'When it was discovered that the 747 had been tampered with,'" he began, "'and the airspeed sensors had been removed to cut corners, an international team of police led by Interpol stepped up efforts to track down the criminals, who were clearly in violation of international laws and responsible for putting the lives of passengers and crew at grave risk. Interpol, assisted by the remarkable efforts of decorated U.S. pilot Gene Coyle, found the owners of the 747 on Penang Island, where they were arrested, tried, convicted and sentenced to long prison terms.'"

Jake stopped reading and looked at his wife, Lily, who wiped away tears from her eyes, reminded once again how close she had come to losing her son, her husband, and so many friends.

"Look how it catches the light!" A.D. said, breaking the spell. Her voice was both awestruck and joyful, as she looked over the railing at the display built just for the rose crystal.

"You know," Carly said to Mack and A.D., "you really didn't have to give both crystals over to the museum. One of them could have come in handy someday!"

A.D. came over and gave Carly a sisterly hug. Of all the friendships that been formed by the events leading up to the near-crash of the 747, it was probably A.D. and Carly's friendship that was the strongest.

"Well," Mack said, "I gave mine to the museum on the condition that I could borrow it whenever I needed it. To tell you the truth, I honestly don't know what I'd do with it right now."

As he spoke, Mack's mom looked on and shook her head, saying, "I don't think any of us can handle another global adventure powered by those crystals. So I for one am glad to see them in a locked display case at America's most secure museum."

Two armed museum guards who were flanking the crystals nodded confidently in agreement, one of them pointing to a computer-encoded laser alarm system that had been installed just for this display.

"Just look at what they ended up saying about the crystals," Mack said with a sigh after reading the plaque. "It's pathetic. The top scientists in the world can't explain what happened. Even after all the interviews they did of me and Dad and all their research, all they could do was explain the *history* of the crystal's powers… not how it worked."

A.D. just smiled calmly and knowingly, shrugging her shoulders as she winked at Mack.

"Good pictures of Evers, though," Jake said, as he looked at the photos of his father on display. He recognized some from old family photo albums, only they were blown up to exhibition size. "Man, what an adventure his life was. What a great man…"

One photo captured Evers as a young man in his jungle outfit, holding a machete in one hand and clutching the rose crystal in the other. Another picture showed Evers as a much older man standing with Mack in his attic study on Martha's Vineyard. He was holding up a bone talisman, looking very much like the wise teacher he had become.

And now, standing there at the Smithsonian and looking at his Dad's face, Mack noticed a sense of respect for Evers that he had never seen before from Jake for his Dad.

The museum's P.A. system squawked to life and barked out a loud message: "The special viewing of the Rose Crystal Exhibit at the Smithsonian Air and Space museum is now closing. Family and friends of the exhibit and honored guests are asked to please depart the museum at this time and board the courtesy bus for an historic and educational tour of the city, narrated by Mr. Bates…"

The kids all collectively groaned with disappointment …until the voice on the P.A. continued:

"…followed by the distribution of the commemorative 747 Lego kits, courtesy of the Lego Company, which had them flown in from their corporate headquarters in Denmark this afternoon."

The cheers and near stampede that followed were deafening, followed by an actual *whoosh* as the kids all rushed to the doors and boarded the bus, Harry leading the charge.

With the bus loaded, including Jake, Lily, and A.D., it rolled toward the Capitol building, where it would stop briefly before heading to the airport to pick up the goodies. The Smithsonian was locked up behind them, and the newly installed laser alarms activated.

Shortly after they left, Jake's pager went off. But it was an odd and unfamiliar beep, not the dreaded crash-alert tone; this was something new. Jake breathlessly read the message on his pager. He looked up in astonishment, unable to speak. He passed the pager to Lily, whose face went a little pale. She passed it to A.D., who read the message and started laughing uproariously.

Finally, Mack and Carly got a chance to see the message, and Mack read it aloud to Harry and everyone else on the bus:

NEWS FLASH: MAGIC ROSE CRYSTALS STOLEN FROM SMITHSONIAN EXHIBIT. LASER ALARMS MYSTERIOUSLY DISARMED. WITNESSES SAY TWO THIEVES IN EXOTIC BEJEWELED CLOAKS SEEM TO HAVE VANISHED INTO THIN AIR.

* * * THE END * * *

Made in the USA
Lexington, KY
29 February 2012